HEROES DON'T ALWAYS WEAR CAPES

HEROES DON'T ALWAYS WEAR CAPES

Stefania Shaffer

Pressman Books

2005

For Marty —
Thank you
for believing
in me — always!
And for your
help — belong the
way. Wishing you
many happy readings!

Stefania Shaffer

HEROES DON'T ALWAYS WEAR CAPES
Copyright © 2006 Stefania Shaffer
Pressman Books

For more information about this title, please contact:
Pressman Books
P.O. Box 1827
Woodbridge, CA 95258-1827
www.pressmanbooks.com

Book design by:
Arbor Books
www.arborbooks.com

Printed in the United States

Stefania Shaffer
HEROES DON'T ALWAYS WEAR CAPES

Library of Congress Control Number: 2005907554
ISBN: 0-9772325-0-6

For the mother of Molly Morene Klecka,
I am eternally grateful to you.

To my Sister-Friends, Tonja, who held the door open so I could
walk through it to a brighter future,

…and Aimee, who held my hand every step of the way while
writing this book.

For Jenene, and for Larry, my real life "Gus-Gus," whose constant
cheering-on planted the thought that maybe I could.

And to my Gordon, your gentle and final words, "What are you
waiting for?", have led me to, "I did it!"

Acknowledgements

A book is not a book without the many hands it passes through.

The creative team at Arbor Books created the stunning art design for the cover. My immense thanks to Larry, Dennis, Maria, and Calvin who spent countless hours detailing every shade of red until the perfect ruby was unveiled. Without their talent, you would not have picked up this book.

My publishers Larry and Joel gave me every reason to trust that I am in good hands. That special brand of New York energy dazzled me in my very first conversation with Larry, and has kept me smiling throughout the process, sizzling with new ideas after every exchange.

My extremely meticulous editor Andrew put tender loving care into his reading as evidenced in his comments to me. His ability insured that what I meant to say and what I did say are not two different things.

To my gentle readers who laughed in all the right places, and encouraged me to go on, even after they gave me their two cents on the first twenty pages: Angela, Kathy, Aimee, Tonja, Larry, and Gordon. Additionally, for Tracy, and Audrey, who loved it even more when it was finished, thank you for your exuberance. Special thanks to those here who also endorsed the completed work, especially Dr. McCaffrey.

To those who taught me how to handle rejection in the earliest stage of my sales career: Jack, Cliff and Steve. With every early rejection letter for this book, I smiled knowing I was one step closer to "yes."

Finally, for the real heroes I had in mind while spinning this tale: Sally Ryan, Doris Schreiber, and Michael McKenna. Your impact helped to shape the adult I became and, in turn, I try to honor your lessons as I pass them on to my own students.

HEROES DON'T ALWAYS WEAR CAPES

Meeting Vandra Zandinski

Chapter 1

"What do you know about children, Ms. ... Zaniski, is it?"

After slaughtering my name, she never gets it right, I want to stop the interview right here and ask her exactly why it is that people who are trying to adopt children must be subjected to these impossible inquisitions. Why must I be made to explain away my life, when the fifteen-year-old at the end of my street is raising her baby and getting financial support to do so? Did anyone ask <u>her</u> what <u>she</u> knows about mothering?

This is my first face-to-face interview with Barbara Sanders. She is a cold woman who speaks in an affected, upstate New England accent. Her cropped auburn hair sets off her doe eyes and swan-like neck. She reminds me of a ballet matron interviewing me for an apprenticeship.

In our prior telephone conversations, that run more like ask-and-answer sessions on C-SPAN, I have been asked to chisel away the meanings behind any philosophy I have ever ascribed to, any bumper sticker I have ever brandished, and state, with certainty, the political votes I have cast in every election since I turned eighteen. Did I vote in every election? What makes me a model citizen?

I have filled out paperwork, reams and reams of paperwork, about my health, physical and mental, and degenerative illnesses that run in my family. How can I answer what I do not know? When I was growing up, I only received a little piece of paper that stated the romanticized version of how I was conceived, and that my biological mother wanted a better life for me; one that, as a college student studying art, she could not provide herself.

I have listed hundreds of references that even top-level security cleared government officials aren't required to provide. I must show without a doubt that I will be able to raise a child in this changing world of moral values and new dangers and general apathy; that my superb sensibilities will propel this youngster into a stratosphere that leaves all the other children being raised by equally good and decent, and loving and caring, parents behind.

While I am frustrated about, and nearly incensed by, the process that has invaded every inch of my personal space, I am equally thrilled that I have made it thus far. This is the next step in the application process to adopt a little bundle of joy. My girlfriends and I are all at the stage in our lives now where college is a distant memory, and anniversaries with our husbands still bring a little hopefulness that maybe this will be the year we can turn the guest room into a nursery. Nobody really comes to stay anymore anyway.

We are all a little busier trying to manage the amount of possessions we have accumulated with dual incomes. It's amazing how we think we can fill the empty voids in our lives with great cars, a new stuffed armchair or items we only used once before rewrapping and packing away on one of the shelves in our gift closet.

"Ms. Zaniski? If you could answer the question. What do you know about children that will make you fit to be a mother?" Her pen in hand stands at attention, ready to take down my answer in shorthand. How can she possibly write down everything I have to say about what I know of raising children?

I remember all of those times where I relied on the help of an adult to get me through some really difficult experiences. I know I can be an effective adult role model to any child because of the compassion someone else showed me. But this answer is too clipped. I need this woman to really know that I have learned some pretty big lessons in life and, if I can pass them along to my child, she will become a stellar individual.

I try to casually glance at the form she is waiting to fill out, depending upon my response. I believe I can see two boxes. I wonder if the instructions read, "Please indicate whether this woman understands the role adults play in the lives of children, and if her knowledge of children deems her a worthy candidate for our next available baby. Check "yes" or "no."

I swallow. I breathe deeply. And I begin in the sweetest, most poised, yet confident, manner I know. "Mrs. Sanders, it's Zandinski, not Zaniski. Don't worry, lots of people have trouble with it. I tell them, 'That's okay. It's one of those names you'll either never forget or never get right.'" I am trying to lighten the tension in here. "If it's easier, please just call me Vandra."

"Very well, Vandra. What do you know about children?"

"Well, aside from the fact that I was one, I remember vividly many pivotal experiences that shaped who I became. I remember the loneliness that children feel sometimes when things aren't going right at home. I remember the thrill that children get when their dad comes home early from work to take them looking for salamanders in the rain. I remember the hopefulness that maybe this will be the day that there are freshly baked cookies waiting for me.

"I remember adults who were kind to me, and not so kind to me, and I vowed that I would never forget these lessons as I became a grownup. I have the richness of a dozen or so strong role models etched in my heart.

"What I know about children is that they want to be loved, and they want to have boundaries. They are not looking for material items to make them happy. They are looking for recognition of their achievements.

"And nothing makes a child feel more special than knowing some adult who saw a little spark of potential there went out of their way to help hone that into a talent."

"I would like to know some specific details about particular lessons you say you have learned. How will these make your child better able to handle life's difficulties? Can you please tell me about the people who, as you say, impacted you in your youth?"

I know there is no way she will be able to write down everything I am about to share. But I also know she will only need to walk away with a general impression. Check "yes" or "no." So, I start from the beginning.

Preschool with Sister Mary-Catherine

There is nothing a child looks forward to more than the first day of school. Unless, of course, you're me and it happens to be the first time in your life you are ripped from the arms of the only caretakers you've known and catapulted into a large room, covered in pastel peach paint, where you will be forced to make new friends and learn how to tie your shoes.

I am not a fan of preschool; Montessori, as it is known. I believe this name is a philosophy behind its education, as well as a title for kinder care. This experience is my first introduction to the world of nunneries. Women, all quite unattractive, are dressed in heavy black robes and wearing habits to hide their hair-don'ts. These are not inviting images to a little girl who likes to play with pretty Barbie dolls and watch pretty ladies on television, as I am accustomed to doing after having been indoctrinated into the fine drama of daytime television through my mother's addiction to "Days of Our Lives."

As I approach my first day, I am under the impression this is a place my mother will be attending with me. This is a false impression, and, more accurately, a tightly spun web of lies to create a scenario that will lure me out the door and into the station wagon. I am four years old, but I am independent and single-minded. I have a strong desire to stay home and find out what happens to Susan, the beautiful Susan Hayward on my regular soap. I am far more interested in fictitious characters than I am in the reality awaiting me at Montessori.

But, here I stand, shrieking and sobbing, and making quite a spectacle of myself. I am too shy at the thought of walking over to introduce myself, so instead I aim for the less obvious approach; I announce my arrival at the front door with a bloodcurdling scream.

My decibel level is ill-befitting anyone over the age of two who is not planted dead center of a Toys 'R Us aisle, clutching desperately a new "Barbie Goes to the Beach" outfit, which is now only a bent-up piece of cardboard, squeezed in a choke hold by little fingers wrapped tightly around it.

It's not as if my mother isn't accustomed to a good, crowd pleasing spectacle, for which she, herself, has become known. She has somewhat of a rhythm for creating some bloodcurdling screams anywhere she deems appropriate: the grocery store, the church parking lot, the public library. She always blames it on us kids. Calling us for dinner. Calling us to the car. Calling us from a quiet fabric store by standing in the middle of the room, keys held high in the air, jingling wildly.

At the sound of this signal, we are to either all come directly to her at once, so she can do a head count before heading to the car, or until she spies us outside the glass door, away from strangers who might associate us with this unabashed woman. The looming threat is always repeated before we head out on these little excursions: "If you don't come when I call you, I'm leaving you behind." One time, she didn't see me through the other side of the glass door I scampered to when I heard those keys begin to bellow. I finally made it to the car just as she began revving up the engine.

The keys are never very subtle in the sound they make, as steel clanks anxiously upon steel. My mother carries a ring of keys that would put any self-respecting janitor to shame. The heaping mass of tin weighs down her purse so heavily that even with her lack of athletic prowess she can hurl that carpetbag like a lead propelled balloon and nail one of my brothers in the back, knocking him flat to the cement.

This is always her first move. If you get out of line, she'll take the wind out of you long enough to get you in slow motion. You'll find yourself on the ground, wheezing, counting the minutes before she gets close. She never runs. This trick gives her just enough time to catch up to however far you may have dashed off.

So, my mother is very used to spectacles, having masterminded a few in her day. The one I am gainfully immersed in now is not at all of the caliber to register any kind of response from her, other than to go ahead with her morning plans of dropping me off and expecting Sister Mary-Catherine to deal with me the way she had lovingly helped other tots acclimate to their first day of school. And so she leaves.

Here I am. Alone. No one has come to my rescue, and no one seems bothered that this little girl in her peach gingham romper is seemingly uncomfortable with the idea of venturing inside. Sister Mary-Catherine gives it a go.

She is an old nun. She has a face that blends with the other faces, tucked under the habits that all of the nuns wear, and spectacles that only frame her gray eyes with a rim of white metal. Perhaps she was a blonde in her youth. I only know that she is now definitely gray, as measured in the tint of her furrowing brows that match the single strand of hair coiling from her chin.

"Would you like to come in and join the other children?" are the only words with which she greets me. Can't anybody see I am in need of a tissue?

"I w-want m-my M-mom-mmmy!" I manage to howl through labored breathing.

"Sorry, but you're Mommy has gone for a little while and she has left you here with us. You may sit outside here on the porch until you collect yourself and can be part of the group." There is no negotiating with this nun. She's had it. My tantrum does not work as well as the ones I have seen my mother throw. We always come running, gushing over her, hoping one of us will offer some clever remark to cheer her miserable disposition right up before dad gets home from work.

But alas, it seems like a nice day, and there are some really big swing sets on the lawn, so I decide to stay outside until I feel I can join the rest of the group. I don't think this makes a very good impression on Sister Mary-Catherine. I also think it leads to my later difficulties of being labeled a troublemaker and, thus, having to do penance in the secret room.

What I do come to like at Montessori isn't in the group play or the floor map that helps us learn our states or the xylophone that you get to play if you can spell its name, nor does my enjoyment stem from the indoor jungle gym which, in theory, teaches us how to interact with others while using our imagination to create and pretend. No. My favorite part of Montessori is free time, where I can conveniently find an excuse to roam nearest to Eric Webb.

I don't pay enough attention to know if there are any other boys in this preschool. It may well be all girls, except for the delightful, Nordic Eric Webb. He has crinkly eyes that you can tell are navy blue when he isn't smiling. As soon as you make him laugh, which he does easily, his eyes will disappear inside masses of bushy blond lashes that go on for days. How is it that girls are never blessed with these kinds of assets? Eric is my only friend.

There is another girl, whose house I used to visit when our mothers wanted to have deep conversations away from all of the other mothers, but I stopped going to visit her after the last time when, upon patiently listening to the details of the next tea date to be set, I couldn't hold it any longer and accidentally peed standing up while waiting in the living room for my mother to take me home.

Even with this faux pas, I still consider myself delicate enough to catch the attention of Eric Webb and the wantonness that lurks within him, even as a four-year-old. He always wears this mischievous grin that looks like he has just done something that will take you a long while to guess, or that he has a splendid idea to share about something that can be done, if we are very, very careful. I like him a lot.

But Sister Mary-Catherine does not like the idea that I like boys. I think she is rather horrified at the idea that I am turning out to be a little too independent for her taste. After all, they do not breed independent thinking at Montessori if it means that your individualism goes against the grain of the Montessori cloth. Apparently, my individualism is standing out among the other independent thinkers in training. As far as I can tell, I am getting on exceedingly well. I am making choices—choosing to stay outside on my first day to enjoy the sun and a good round on the swings—I am making friends. Is there a rule against boyfriends in preschool?

After some time of nourishing my wanderlust by engaging in as many conversations about soldiers and robots and scandalous ideas of what to do to the nuns, as Eric and I can carry on, I start to get a sense that the nuns are watching me. If I play on the jungle gym and relinquish the decision making to the other children of what imaginary building the fortress will become today, I still sense that I have somehow done something to warrant gazing eyes upon me.

I start to feel uncomfortable. I mosey on over to the xylophone, spell out "x-y-l-o-p-h-o-n-e," thereby being allowed to play. Lurkers are about, just watching me. What is the conspiracy? I am only four. Can it be that I actually am single-handedly ruining the minds of the other independent thinkers in training? So I stroke the xylophone with the fuzzy gavel and try my best to play a little musical tune that sounds somewhat familiar to me, until I am interrupted by the approaching nuns, whom I can see out of the corner of my eye. This is the first time I learn the term "peripheral vision."

"Child, please step into the viewing room with us. We'd like to have a word with you." Nothing about these words brings me any comfort. I feel as though I have done something sinful. Furthermore, what is the "viewing room?"

So, I trail behind the long flowing masses of black fabric that practically shield me from the view of the other children as we head around the corner from the xylophone and the glorious wall mirror hanging above.

I peek over my shoulder to scan the room for Eric Webb and I only see a tussle of blond bed head bobbing, as the person attached beneath is flying marine pilots into enemy territory. I am alone. Even Eric Webb can't save me now. He is engaged in war with Jeffrey Thomas. His pilots are fighting for their lives as they try to deflect one bomb after another.

The secret room lies hidden behind the two-way glass that is covered by a long wall mirror fitted above the xylophone. It is a viewing arena that can fit four nuns and one bad child at a time.

This is the purest form of intimidation. Isolate the child in a room full of scowling nuns who hover over the poor victim in a standing position of three feet above. This forces the child into submission purely by use of a horizontal strategy. The child is made to look up, while wrenching her neck backward into a most unnatural pose. The child will then admit to almost anything in order to alleviate the tension and pain and near dizziness caused by this wretched position.

"It has come to our attention, Missy, that you are distracting the others from learning and creating by stifling their imagination with your own vision," Sister Mary-Catherine begins. In a way, I think this is meant as a compliment. Aren't they, in actuality, telling me that I show great leadership potential as I share my distinct vision with other playmates and that they, in turn, buy into my ideas and play along? The only problem I can see is that my name is not Missy. Is it possible they have me confused with some other deserving little girl who should actually be behind this glass veneer? Surely there should be some other innocent child out there being made to feel guilty for something she wrongfully did unwittingly. It couldn't be me. This must be some case of mistaken identity. Is the nun brigade sure they were observing the right party, wrongfully placed in front of this firing squad?

"Furthermore, we have been watching your interactions with one of our brightest young students and find that you are monopolizing his time to grow and experience individually the philosophies behind Montessori's school of learning. Eric Webb needs to engage in role-playing with other peers who express similar interests. These activities typically include war games, where boys can simulate what it will be like to grow into responsible men one day. They must focus on strategic maneuvers, and distractions from on-looking little girls can be cause for errors in judgment," Sister Mary-Catherine continued.

I am not sure what she is saying, but, again, it sounds to me as if she might be complimenting me for my astuteness at recognizing brilliance in the room, and seeking after it. After all, she identified Eric as the smartest child in our group. That must make me at least the second smartest because I picked him to be my best friend. In fact, I have selected him to be my husband. But I think I will save this information for later.

"We have also observed that some of your skills are not yet on a par with the other students, and by now, you should be proficient at lacing and tying your shoes—both of them." It went on. "Our decision has been discussed by all the nuns, and we are in agreement that your free time will be restricted until you are able to master tying your shoes, both of them, within the appropriate time limit expected. Until you can achieve this level of performance, you are not to be swirling about Eric Webb, nor guiding any of the other children on the Eiffel Tower tour of the jungle gym. You will not be allowed to swing outdoors, nor play with paints, and certainly not allowed to play the xylophone. And, perhaps, you will not be invited to sit in the learning circle when Smoky the Bear comes to visit on Friday, unless you have mastered tying your shoes, both of them." It ended there. Almost.

"Well, Missy, do you understand what we are saying?" she leers into my line of vision so close I could snap her nose off with one bite if I was the lunging sort of child. However, I know this is not the answer to my problem, particularly since I am behind the secret wall where only bad children are taken, and no one will be able to hear me scream. And so I am defeated.

I begin to feel my bottom lip push out and quiver uncontrollably. The sad, turned down smile is beginning to force its way onto my face. I do not want to cry. I do not want this nun to know she has hurt me beyond belief. I do not want her to know that I have actually begun to enjoy Montessori and that I have forgotten all about "Days of Our Lives" and my mother's irate escapades.

I do not want to tell her that the only joy I have each day for four hours is coming to see my best friend, whom I love. He is the smartest person I know, and I know how to make him laugh. We were fast friends, and now Sister Mary-Catherine is trying her hardest to make me feel that I am inhibiting Eric Webb's learning ability, intimating that I am somehow not the right kind of influence on him. She practically makes me feel that I am destroying his genius. He doesn't seem to mind.

I can only stand there and silently sob. This is the saddest kind of cry because it is the most heart wrenching. It is impossible to release the pain when there is no sound coming out. When we stifle our sadness, our lungs hurt a little more, and the pit of our tummy feels like everything bad is being stuffed down into it. It's like trying to breathe while learning the freestyle stroke, but gulping in a huge gallon of chlorinated water instead of the much needed breath you are intending to take. It hurts, and chokes, and makes the pain so much greater because everything that should be coming out is going in.

Finally, Sister Mary-Catherine puts her wrinkled and knotted fingers on my shoulder, as if to pat me, but it was more to hold me in place, while she asks me again, "Missy, do you understand what is expected of you at Montessori?"

I can only reply, "My name is not Missy. It's Vandra Zandinski," which lands me with another choice to make. Of course, not the one I would have liked. That would have been too easy. Had the question been, "Would you like to leave the Montessori or stay with the group?" I would have clearly chosen to stay, because anywhere near Eric Webb is better than any other option I have waiting for me at home. However, the question remains, "Would you like to sit in here or go outside until you can return to the group?"

So, for the second time this year, I choose to go it alone outside with only my sadness to comfort me. I may not have learned the states this year or found the right melody on that xylophone. I surely did not get the time needed to discover my inner Picasso or to round up tour groups to continue the guided experiences I would lead of the Eiffel Tower, or the caves beneath the sea that I vividly constructed out of our indoor jungle gym parts and some imaginary walls. But I do learn to tie my shoes, both of them, within the acceptable one-minute limit.

And I learn something else that only Sister Mary-Catherine can teach me. In her own way, she spelled out for me the difference between being a winner and being a bad influence. It doesn't have much to do with your knowledge base; it has everything to do with perception and first impressions.

Once you set foot on new terrain in front of a crowd, you are being judged and labeled. Right or wrong, this makes it easier for people to identify you.

Independent thinkers who follow our rules fit nicely over here with the other children who are awaiting instruction on how to proceed in self-discovery.

Independent thinkers who outsmart the group, rise to the top and are allowed to play war games and receive other special privileges, while getting away with bloody murder behind the scenes so long as another person can be called the scapegoat.

Independent thinkers who choose the unpopular answers, who do not conform, who have loud and brash mothers, who take charge where it appears the masses will not, are carefully examined, and when the evaluation is complete, your achievements will either be overlooked, underplayed, ignored entirely or, in the rare instance, held up as a competitive example to emulate.

In my case, Sister Mary-Catherine only inspires me to work harder at creating a better first impression so that I will be given opportunities in the future to prove that I am a worthy contender to lead and be followed.

Kindergarten with
Mrs. Hayworth

While the nuns at Montessori were an excellent precursor to all that I would surely encounter again in adulthood, the experience does not sour me on furthering my education in kindergarten. In fact, I am quite excited, this time, to enter a higher state of learning. I get to be on campus with big kids. And I know that when their lunch is beginning, I can still go home to enjoy "Days of Our Lives" and work on the quilts my mother is patchworking from scraps of Toughskin jeans my brothers are famous for wearing out within two weeks.

Any mother of active boys knows that buying clothes is a particular dilemma, especially pants. Calculating the child's growth spurts while remembering just how many baseball game practices one pair will weather is a chore. A mother has to really crunch some numbers in order to determine just how many pairs of these miracle material trousers she can buy without breaking her esteemed reputation for being thrifty with her husband's paycheck. The recommended replacement time for a regular pair of Toughskin jeans for any boy averaging regular wear and tear is six weeks. It says so on the guarantee. However, I don't think the makers of Toughskins had my brothers in mind when they put a label right on the pants that says, "Money back if you're not satisfied."

My brothers practically torment their pants in the first weekend of play to the point that they can not pass them off for suitable church wear the next day. While my mother takes great pleasure in dressing my sister and I in ruffles and bows, the only look she seems to pull together for my brothers is "clean."

By the time a full school week has passed, the Toughskins are beginning to show significant signs of fading in the trademark fabric that is guaranteed to hold its color. The dye lots are obvious choices from a marketing standpoint. Brown, for rolling in dirt; burgundy, for the one or two occasions that might require stitches after nearly bleeding to death; and green, the ever popular color for sliding in wet grass. I am not sure what the purpose is for navy. Perhaps it is intended for church only.

Sears, Roebuck becomes a Friday night ritual for us every other week, when my father gets paid. If all four of us children can manage to pile into the station wagon peacefully enough, without anyone throwing a tantrum or getting lost in the store, then our big reward awaiting us at the end is the free popcorn encased in a little striped red bag that wears the words "Thank you for shopping Sears" emblazoned across the front. All along the bottom of the bag, and creeping up the sides, is a splattering of butter grease beginning to seep through. This is how we know it is freshly made. The more butter we can see through the bag, the hotter it is and, therefore, the fresher it must be. We didn't know there was a popcorn light that remained on at all times. That bulb was there to keep kids like us coming back for more. We wanted as much of that fresh buttery taste we could get, even if it had been sitting there since the four o'clock snack hour for everyone in the Maytag Appliance department to raid.

The patchwork quilt I am dutifully looking forward to making with my mother is a chore in itself for two reasons: I am not allowed to talk, unless it is during the commercial break from our popular soap; and it is incredibly difficult to pierce Toughskin swatches with a thickly threaded needle of yarn. My brothers can conquer the unimaginable feat of breaking through the Toughskins guarantee by shredding their knees within two weeks, but I can't seem to break through one stitch without piercing my fingers and leaving bloodstains on the fabric. Fortunately, it is the burgundy, which is intended for such accidents. When I finally accomplish this one great task, I say, "Look, Mommy, I did it. Aren't you proud?"

To which the reply is invariably, "Shhhhh. Wait until a commercial break."

Kindergarten will be a wonderful transition to my inevitable growing up and moving away from home. It will be better than the experience at Montessori with the nuns because I will know a lot of other kids from my neighborhood. I will have immediate friends and we will all play together and everybody will like me.

My hopes are dashed on the first day. I did not realize there would be two kindergarten classes. Children are being sorted into classes in a most unconventional way. We all stand on a painted line in front of both classroom doors at precisely 8 a.m. Each teacher has a roll sheet for scooting in the next little genius. They call our names aloud as each group of friends stands panicked, clasping hands tightly, as if trying to signal to the teachers, "We are friends and we need to stay together."

I know Miss Larkin is going to be my teacher. She is young and blond. Her hair is long, like every other woman in the early 1970s. She has a great big Pearl Drops toothpaste smile and she radiates. I can tell she loves children because she is practically caressing the backpacks as they move across her threshold into a classroom that is not merely textiled in green chalkboards and alphabet symbols and days of the week to memorize, it is spilling over with an intoxicating aroma. I call it "the joy of learning."

This is going to be a happy year for me. I can tell right away that Miss Larkin and I click. Even though we have not, as yet, shaken hands or exchanged exuberant smiles, I can feel her radiance and I know I will learn more from her than any other teacher in the whole world. I also notice that a lot of the cool kids in the neighborhood, who have really cool older brothers or sisters, are going into Miss Larkin's class. This just reaffirms to me my astute decision making ability that it will be a kindergarten year filled with fast friends, a fun teacher and forever the joy of learning instilled in me.

I don't have my special group of friends to hold my hand. They are already being called in to class. But, my mom is here with me. Near me. Just outside the bicycle gate, looking on from the ramp that borders the playground. She can tell, with a squint, that I am still standing upon the yellow line waiting, and waiting, and waiting to be called.

It happens. Finally, the "Zs." But, it isn't Miss Larkin's sweet sing-song voice that I hear saying my name. It is the other teacher's, Mrs. Hayworth. I start to cry. Right then and there. I am so disappointed. Doesn't anybody notice that my group of really cool friends that I want so badly to meet has already been invited into the other class? They are surely waiting for me, saving me a seat, begging for me to eat my snack with them. How is it possible that I have to go alone to Mrs. Hayworth's and experience Sister Mary-Catherine all over again?

Just to glance at Mrs. Hayworth I can tell she is the kind of teacher who has been at it a long time, and probably more accurately put, too long. She is round and short. She has a pair of half-dome eyeglasses hanging by a chain around her neck and a fully round-sized pair seated upon her nose. She has frail hair that winds into neat rows of curls, the kind that look like she sleeps on foam curlers with a hair net. She wears an apron. This makes her look more grandmotherly, but not in a welcoming way. She does not appear to be the type to have a warm batch of cookies pulled freshly from the oven upon the arrival of small guests. She appears to be the disheveled kind. In a kitchen, during baking season, she would be more apt to dust flour from her face while simultaneously shooing away cats who meander across countertops; cats who leave remnants of their fur inside the dough as they swish their tails defiantly in response to her effortless, "Scats."

"She was due to retire in June, but decided to extend her stay one more year," is what some of the mothers behind me are saying while the majority of kids are still awaiting their destiny. Just my luck. A teacher whose apparent "joy of learning" is not covering her classroom walls. Instead, I arrive to find a smattering of numbers pinned to the wall in order from 1 to 100; I find cursive alphabet strips so we can easily recognize the proper way to write in D'Nealian hand; I find a teacher's desk cluttered with manila folders that are records of all her new students. What does mine say about my stint with the nuns?

Hat and coat still on, I lean against the wall-length cupboards to take in my surroundings. Bare walls painted in eggshell white beg to hang dazzling artwork that only kindergartners know how to finger-paint. A few lockers hold our winter coats, and a changing room, for any one who wets their pants while at school, is hidden behind a moveable curtain wall. Nothing enticing. Nothing that shouts, "Welcome, students. Don't be afraid. We're all going to have a fabulous year together!"

Through wet lashes, I look to my teacher for any instructions. Mrs. Hayworth directs us to sit upon the floor. "There is no particular order," she says, so I sit next to another little girl who looks equally displeased to be here, but mostly because she looks like she isn't even awake yet. She is sucking her thumb and her hair hasn't been brushed. Other than that, she is wholly unaware of the travesty about to ensue in Mrs. Hayworth's room simply because we didn't get placed in Miss Larkin's class.

Mrs. Hayworth wants to know if there is anything special about us. What do we like to do? What is our favorite color? Candy? Who is a person we like best? We are to give some kind of information along with our name, and how we pronounce it, so everyone can stare at us. Mrs. Hayworth sits upon her chair, which rolls from her desk to the center of the room, where we are seated upon carpet tiles. Her chair was once upholstered in fine black leather, but it now has one long strip dangling from the seat, exposing the under-stuffing, which is a honey-colored foam. Why doesn't she just cut that strip off? Is she planning to reattach it with a needle and thread or some Scotch tape, or even a staple or two? By the look of it, that chair was planning to retire last year, too.

"Hi. I'm Brad Hamilton. I don't like to be called Bradley. I like to watch the 49ers cream the Raiders, and my dad got me an autographed football from Joe Namath!" goes the first kid. He seems pretty self-confident, especially for a five-year-old.

"I'm Monique," the little doe-eyed blonde barely whispered. "I love to swim." What did she say? None of us can make out anything she mumbled because she was practically talking to herself, with her chin down and no audible sounds of emission.

"Tell us again, dear. What is it you like to do?" Mrs. Hayworth pleasantly probes.

"I like to swim," comes out even softer and more unsure than the first time. I can see that this girl is going to need some help in a serious way. She is beyond shy, and now we are beginning to see the crack of a boo-boo face coming on. I hope Mrs. Hayworth will just let it go.

"Dear, we can't quite understand you. You'll have to speak up. Don't be afraid. I'm not going to bite you." I am not so sure about that.

The rows of children rate their favorite hobbies and colors and homemade cookies and places to visit and first books they've already read. Then Mrs. Hayworth gets to me. "Dear, what is it that is special about you?"

I'm sure she doesn't mean it the way it comes out. I certainly know this is the topic we are discussing, but knowing that I did not get selected for Miss Larkin's class makes me feel not very special today. Remembering that all I tried to do last year at Montessori was to show some initiative and leadership, and now there is a folder sitting atop Mrs. Hayworth's desk with my name on it. Wondering what's inside makes me feel uneasy. I stumble for a clever answer, but I am not very assured that teachers like my clever answers. So I am honest. "I'm sure there is something special about me, but I don't know exactly what it is right now."

Mrs. Hayworth looks at me puzzled. She can't tell if she should take pity on me or scold me for mocking her assigned question. I answered with such bravado that I don't come across as very pitiful, so she deems me as rather defiant; at the very least, an unusual child that she will need to watch carefully. A feeling of doom passes over me.

Suddenly, a jingling bell clangs outside our doors. An older child arrives pushing a cart. The happiest time of kindergarten happens when the milk monitor calls my name. For ten cents I can have a cold carton with a straw, and thirty minutes to rest. I take my nap and fall asleep hard. There is no wind down time for me. I do not need to be soothed by the strings of Mozart. I don't even complain that there is not one mat left for me to lie upon. I have my blanky and my empty carton beside me, and nothing but the purest milk breath can put me out of my misery and into a coma-like sleep.

In my first day of kindergarten, I learn from Mrs. Hayworth that many times we will have a moment to reflect upon our circumstances, and that taking a nap can always help us regain the strength we need to look at the same picture with fresh eyes, to get a new perspective.

We won't always get to be with the in-crowd. A teacher who looks old and scattered, very well is old and scattered.

I learn this year that Mrs. Hayworth is also impatient with little children, and particularly impatient with me. She rarely smiles and, worst of all, instead of joy in my first year, she puts a fear of learning into me that will take years to undo.

More than anything, I learn that we sometimes feel a very real connection to strangers for unexplained reasons, and that it is sometimes better to pursue these karmic meetings rather than wonder about what might have been. I still wonder what the students in Miss Larkin's class learned without me.

First Grade with Miss Parsons

Oh, "Joy to the World." It is not only the hit song on the radio, but it seems to be the ode to Miss Parsons. Her first name is Joy, and she is jubilant. She is my first pretty teacher, and her love for all children is cast upon us daily. It is, after all, the era of free love, so I figure Miss Parsons is just caught up in the movement. She radiates. Every day. But it is really her hair that keeps us all entranced. It is long and glossy. It dips at the end of her waist, and some days, when she wears it down, it slinks across the desk as she bends over to help me with my first spelling word list. She can be gone for minutes, and her shampoo scent still lingers. She is the ultimate ad for Wella Balsam shampoo. Some days she wears her hair up, in a tightly twisted French knot that is secured with a single Chinese chopstick, or a number two Ticonderoga pencil.

We always wait for the end of the day. Miss Parson's hair knot will just be coming loose from the rigor of schooling six-year-olds when she decides to take the whole thing down, shake it around a little and then tie it back up. She is a goddess. I know the girls all marvel at her beauty and her graciousness and her patience in teaching us to read. I can't imagine that the boys aren't equally engaged by her scintillating vision, offset by her softly scented tea rose perfume. She makes coming to school a real pleasure; and she brings to me the joy of learning.

It isn't until later that I start to discover that every adult has different sides to them, and that politics in America shapes these adults outside of school. During the early 1970s, the whole role of a woman is being rebelled against and redefined by a nation of younger women who want to be treated equally. My neighborhood becomes a land where my father is constantly trying to shield us from the sight of hippies, braless women or girls in miniskirts hiked up to their navels. Of course, the more he tells us to avert our eyes at the sight of on-comers, the more we look, and look again, while he tries to shuttle us out of evil's path.

Once, I did get an eyeful of a young woman at the grocery store, who was, indeed, wearing a miniskirt hiked up to her navel. The nervousness I felt was a combination of the shame I knew I was supposed to feel for her, mixed with guilt for admiring how she carried herself so confidently. She paraded right by the neighborhood men, who just popped in to pick up a loaf of bread or a gallon of milk in time for 5 o'clock supper. I act stunned, but secretly marvel to know that there are other kinds of women in the world from the images I know. None of the ladies in my neighborhood would be caught dead wearing anything above their knees without girdles and aprons in place.

This modern woman is an image well suited to Miss Parsons. She is a creature of loveliness and has excellent taste in clothes. While they are, indeed, short, most of her dresses are in conservative colors, with white Peter Pan collars to frame her face. On one particular day, Miss Parsons comes to school in a beautiful navy A-line dress that buttons up the front, from hem to neckline. The buttons are daisy appliqués, to match the daisy embroidery clustered around her pointy white collar. Her sleeves are long and flowing and trimmed with white French cuffs that also bear the same daisy detailing topping her neckline. Of course, the hem is near navel level, but somehow the school board overlooks the dress code rules for liberated women.

This day, we sit in our usual reading circle on the floor. It's not a perfect circle. We mostly fall into a little crowd so we can all fill the space on our special reading rug that barely covers one corner of the room. This is one of the activities I look forward to most, because Miss Parsons reads aloud to us and, for a change, I don't have to struggle with the words by myself.

As she walks through the crowd of children on the floor, primly holding her skirt to her sides, she steps around us delicately to get to her special chair, which faces our group. Making her way through the mass of sneakers and little legs that encircle me, she steps over my ankle and slightly loses her balance. As I look up, to be sure she is not going to topple over, I glimpse a side to my teacher I had never seen before. Miss Parsons isn't wearing any underpants.

I learn this day that sometimes a lady who acts like a lady isn't a lady if she forgets to put on her underpants to go to work.

Fourth Grade with Ms. Hirschbein

There seems to be something unsettling about the years that fit between first and fourth grades. This is the time when I discover I cannot read as easily as other children—or "at all," to hear my mother tell it. The after-school homework routine in my house is just about as normal as everyone else's after-school routine in suburbia.

I come home gleefully from the day. I am hungry for a snack. I am curious about what is happening on our soap, "Through the sands of time, these are The Days of Our Lives." I surmise later on, the announcer must have gotten tired of saying the whole title, because it finally becomes shortened to just the latter part, "Days of Our Lives." I am anxiously looking for my mother, who stays at home to take care of us children, so I can tell her about some non-event that seems so exciting to me.

I discover my mother in the living room, reading National Geographic, the only subscription she allows, as it is "informative and a good resource for future school projects." Some mothers wait for their children to step off the bus and walk with them the two blocks home. Some mothers actually walk to school to await their child's dismissal from class, so they can have a leisurely stroll home together. Not my mother. She's a firm believer in teaching me how to be independent and self-sufficient at the age of nine. This is a philosophy that is instilled in me with many lessons ahead in my future.

"Hello. I'm home," I call out with a song in my voice. It's peculiar. For the sixth day in a row, I don't smell cookies fresh out of the oven like Nicole Collins says her mother prepares for her return home each day. Nicole Collins must be a liar. I just don't believe mothers have the time to do these kinds of things when they have valuable information they need to obtain from well-known periodicals about the world's fascinating events and cultures.

I proceed to peer through the living room entry and see her sitting there, my mother. Reveling in her solitude, she is wrapped in a cashmere stole, with her legs folded under her, seated upon the living room sofa, which is really only supposed to be used for guests and church members who come to visit on Sundays. On the occasion church people do drop by unannounced, I find myself squeezing my eyes their tightest as I pray that I might not be embarrassed by the hissy fit my mother is about to throw, or is in the middle of throwing, which is her usual Sunday ritual. Apparently, she does not observe this day as a day of rest, but rather a day of detest.

I move closer, with an expression as if to say, "Didn't you hear me?" when of course, I already know the answer. I remind myself that sometimes Mother doesn't like to be disturbed when she is reading.

She looks up at me, her silver hair framing her face with tufts of curl pinned behind her ears. Her hair reminds me of a farmer's wife, very sensible, short and natural, and nothing fancy about it. Ever.

Her eyes are not blue, nor are they hazel. They are evenly gray, bespeckled with flecks of a woeful spirit permeating through. Her skin is not smooth. It crinkles in the places where her laugh lines are overshadowed by her frown lines. Her lips are not ruby, nor are they lined in anything resembling a beauty routine; they are just dry and in need of wetting often when she speaks. Her cotton mouth is a constant source of urgent requests. "Bring me some more water, Vandra."

"Did you have a good day at school?" starts the familiar inquiry. I know this routine. It's as automatic as my alphabet recitation. I will reply with a long-winded version of something spectacular that happened to me, and she, in turn, will continue to read her National

Geographic, pretending to be interested in what I am saying, but mocking me with each turn of the page.

I feel an anxious flutter coming up from inside me. Somewhere against the back of my throat, words are dying to spew forth to let her know I am here. " I am important. Those children in that village have mothers who at least care enough for them that they stand with them in the mud to make baskets together. Show some interest, woman. I am right here. Make a basket with me," is all I can muster in my head.

Instead, I begin to slide my heels backward, as my chin falls a little closer to the ground, and I shuffle into a retreat from the living room. Before my last step out of view, I throw a backward glance to answer her original question. "It was fine. I have Ms. Hirschbein. She wants us to all practice reading our favorite selection, so we can present aloud in front of class in a month."

"I'm not sure you'll be one of the ones who will be ready in a month. We will have to work every day after school. You know you should be reading much better by now. Colette Collins told me Nicole is already on her sixteenth Nancy Drew book. You should be reading far ahead of her."

It sounds like a good offer, but it never feels very helpful when my mother works with me. My mother gets impatient when she asks me questions about what we just read. I like to think for a minute about an answer that might sound believable before blurting out something completely ridiculous.

I am certain from what I have learned at home, adults do not like it when children are looking upward, as if counting ceiling tiles. I know this because my mother always says this to me as an after-thought while I hold my face still stinging from her swat, trying to keep my bottom lip from trembling. I have concluded that the bot-tom lip is the direct trigger to releasing the water from the tear ducts and a signal to the voice box telling you it is time to release a good long wail of a cry. If I can hold that bottom lip a little longer and avoid the spectacle of blubbering in front of the person who is try-ing to exert power over me, then I can avoid a humiliation deeper than the pain itself. So I try to count seconds. So far, my record time for holding back tears is eighteen seconds. I usually improve by one to two seconds each time the hand strikes. Yesterday, though, I fell back to fourteen, so I am feeling rather victorious right now that I've made it to twenty.

This year the school tries something new with the fourth grade class. It's called a combination, and we are now meeting with the fifth grade class, too. All of the sliding panel doors have been opened between three classrooms so it seems as though we have the size of the playground to run through wildly, if it wouldn't be for tripping over desks and encyclopedia carts positioned in the dead center of our path. I cannot tell if this means I am smart because I am in with the fifth graders or if they are dumb because they are in with me.

My fourth grade teacher is Ms. Hirschbein. She insists we call her Mizzzzz, not Miss, not Mrs. I guess she feels she is too old to be a Miss. She is also not married, and seems to feel that it is not our place to ask why. I can tell she used to be pretty once. I've seen her talking to Miss Parsons in the hall, and it's funny to watch my two teachers together. Ms. Hirschbein is clearly aware that she is not the youngest and prettiest teacher at school anymore. She is probably not even the best-liked, ever since Miss Parsons joined our school. I can tell these things because whenever I see them talk, Miss Parsons smiles a lot and her whole face glows, while Ms. Hirschbein purses her lips and twirls in a huff, her short skirt showing off her chunky thighs.

There are three teachers I rotate through during the day, but Ms. Hirschbein is my main teacher, evidently charged with making sure my reading comes up to grade level. I know there is a bearded man teacher who is in charge of teaching me my digits on a number scale, and other relevant math usage for a nine-year-old. I know there is a blond lady who reminds me of very bland vanilla. Just plain. Her coloring all runs together. She wears shades that make her look like a walking color strip from the paint store with indecisive names like Ecru, Watercress, Eggshell and Cloud written alongside their indistinguishable hues of white.

I move fluidly through my instruction with each of these teachers, but it is largely Ms. Hirschbein whom I credit for helping me to become a better reader. And it isn't because of any one thing she does to work with me. It is only because of the reading group she puts me in where I get to hear Nora Van Houten read aloud.

On Tuesdays, we split into different learning centers. Part of the class goes to the Social Studies room to work on their own paper-mâché globe, part of the class goes to the bearded math teacher for a boring lesson on multiplication tables that is inevitably lost on me because I am more interested in the reasons why he limps, and my part of the class starts with reading group. Today's assignment is from a book called "Into the Woods," which looks sort of scary because on the cover, a girl and a boy are holding hands running through a gloomy forest, looking over their shoulders at the house covered by ivy behind them. Each of us has our own copy of the book, and most of us hate to read, especially in front of others. So we sit as patiently as nine-year-olds can manage for a full forty-five minutes, while each reader takes a turn stumbling over words, skipping lines accidentally, and sometimes just giving up and requesting to go to the bathroom.

Our attention wanes, and some of us are losing our place, until the magical moment when we hear, with perfect pitch, some whistling and whirring. These are the imitated sounds of the wind whipping through the trees as night approaches for Thomas and Becky.

"*Whirrrr, whirrr, whirrr went the winds. Whoooosh went the tops of the trees as they bristled against one another. The skies had changed and darkness was setting in. There was a new smell in the air. Thomas sensed that rain was coming.*

"'*Becky, we're never going to find that skeleton key if we have to come back here tomorrow. We have flashlights. Why don't we go on up ahead to where those lights are coming from? Maybe it's the ranger's place and he can help us. He probably has a phone and we can call our folks, tell them not to worry.' As Thomas spoke, his voice wavered in places that made Becky squeeze his hand even tighter, and walk even slower. She could hear the crackling leaves beneath her as her feet grew heavy and her heart began pushing through her sweater.*"

Nora Van Houten has our attention. She whispers in all the right places. She pounds on the table when she describes the heavy steps of Becky's feet crushing the dried leaves beneath her. She paces her words as if to embody Thomas himself. We can practically see the invisible bead of sweat begin to build atop the furrow of her brow as she reads Thomas' words with mock assurance that it is, indeed, the ranger's house light they can see from the deepness of the dark woods.

My palms are sweating. Nora is the best reader I have ever heard. She has such a command of the words, even the ones she doesn't know. At least I'm pretty sure there must be some words she doesn't know. Am I the only one who doesn't know all of the words on a page?

Nora continues, and we let her. We don't mind giving up our turn a little longer to hear her whisk us through another page. We are riveted. Enraptured. Fully engaged. And, I dare say, inspired. Ms. Hirschbein has done it. She has magically inserted the genius of Nora Van Houten into our little reading group and turned us around. In one single day we aspire to become the second best readers in our group. For truly, we know there will never be one among us who can ever come close to hitting the mark as assuredly as Nora Van Houten.

Ms. Hirschbein may not be the youngest teacher, but she is obviously experienced. I learn from her that, given the right example, any one can be motivated to meet a challenge.

I learn that when you are in the presence of greatness, it's easy to pinpoint the qualities that make a person such a success. Having passion, pausing for dramatic effect to bring your audience in, and speaking with total confidence, no matter what others at the table think of you, are always ingredients for success. Nora already knew this. She may have been a geek, but we all wanted to be just like her that day.

Finally, what I really learn about reading from Ms. Hirschbein this year is that you just can't judge a book by its cover.

Fifth Grade with Miss Ryan

This year is my most pivotal. I finally have a teacher who understands the brilliance that is mine. Miss Ryan has been put here on earth to recognize my potential and to develop it accordingly. And so she does. I put special detail into covering my books and Pee-Chee folders with matching homemade slipcovers. After noticing that I also use color-coded highlighters for each of my subjects, Miss Ryan comes up with a splendid idea. I am put in charge of sick kids.

For any student who is absent on a particular day, I am responsible for getting a manila folder and sticking all the work that we did in class that day into the folder, writing their name on a tab, and then, joy of all joys, delivering it personally to their house after school. I love this part best of all because it saves me from going home to a lonely afternoon, tucked away in my room with only my imagination to play with, for a little while longer.

More importantly, I am good at it. I am the best organizer in fifth grade. Probably the best organizer in the whole school. In fact, I have been into the front office before, where I know secretaries have felt a little sheepish about the mess they keep on their desk when they detect me giving it the once-over. I know, if given the proper tools and a pass out of class during math time, I would be able to straighten and alphabetize any disarray in need of attention. This is what I have been put on earth to do. And I do it with great pride.

Currently, Miss Ryan is wearing her famous kelly green two-piece knit dress. I always admire how she can wear this color so glee-fully, even though some teachers would look like a giant shamrock in it. Not Miss Ryan. She is like Mary Tyler Moore, only with a pixie haircut and a no-nonsense appeal.

I admire, also, how she can manage to get through every day looking so beautiful without a care in the world for the dandruff that builds up along her collar. Some days, this is what I look at most. I wonder why it doesn't fall off her shoulders when she abruptly turns to the chalkboard to explain some other fleeting concept that I can't manage to retain.

I am mesmerized by Miss Ryan. She is the best teacher to explain the rules of the class on the first day of school. I can tell her delivery goes exactly as planned.

"Class, please focus now on the front of the room because you are about to find out what the rules of our class will be for this year. If you do not follow the rules, I will have to send you to the princi-pal's office. And I enjoy having you in my class too much to want to see you spend the rest of your day in the principal's office. So be sure to write these down."

She speaks in a matter-of-fact tone. However, there is always a gleam in her eye that lets us know, even though she means business, there is a really light side to her personality that makes her very lov-able. We never want to disappoint her.

One day, Miss Ryan was not in class when we had all arrived. We always line up outside our door in the hallway, which is inside the building. The first bell rang, and still no sign of Miss Ryan. Four minutes later, the final bell rang, which means that it is 8:30 and we should begin today's spelling warmup. But the only person we saw dashing down the hall was fat old Mr. Kofer, our principal. He is a hairy, red-headed man who reminds me of a muskrat. He has a han-dlebar mustache that makes me wonder if it needs to be combed, just like the bushy hair beneath his hat. The reason why I like to mind Miss Ryan's rules is not because I am afraid to spend time in the principal's office, but merely because I find him to be so utterly hairy and Sasquatch-like that I would have to avert my eyes by counting ceiling tiles, rather than face him to answer any mundane questions about why I couldn't behave myself well enough to stay in class.

"Thank you, class, for waiting so nice and patiently while Miss Ryan is detained. She will be here soon, but I am going to let you inside your class so you can wait in your seats." Mr. Kofer seemed like he was always ready to give a speech. He had a million occasions where he got to speak in public: the library dedication, the introduction of new teachers, the night we bring parents to meet our new teachers, the night we bring parents to view our work at the end of the year, the baseball game when we play against teachers at promotion time. He's always ready to talk, but he always sounds like he's saying the same thing. He is a fancy fellow, but I think he could be a little more friendly, then kids would want to hang out with him in his office. Especially if he trimmed that face beard.

"Now, children, are you familiar with the rules that Miss Ryan has set up for your class? Who can tell me what one of your rules is?" he inquires of us pleadingly, as if he needs to get through this in a hurry and then ditch us for some speech.

"We are not to get out of our seats unless we need to go to the bathroom; and we are not to go to the bathroom unless it is break time," offers Randy, the smart kid everyone makes fun of because he is so dumb. You don't actually tell the adult who is going to leave you alone for a few minutes that you know about the rule that says you can't get out of your seat. Ever.

"Good. That's a fine rule. Can anyone tell me another rule?" Mr. Kofer continues with this method of stalling until he is satisfied that we all remember to sit at our seats, do our work quietly, not throw anything across the room, keep our hands to ourselves and, finally, that if anyone should start bleeding, go next door to get Mrs. Whitehead for help.

Within five minutes, Mr. Kofer departs and we are left to our own devices. As soon as we can no longer hear the echoes of his patent leather penny loafers as they rhythmically click clack across the linoleum floor, down the long corridor that separates us from the fourth graders at the end of the hall, we look at one another from behind our desks. It is a uniform thought we are all sharing. A mischievous grin slides from the corners of our mouths. Even the brainiest students are aglow at the possibilities.

It is clear we know the rules, but without supervision, we are thirty ten-year-olds left to our own devices for who knows how long. The twinkle in Gary Bracht's eyes, the resident troublemaker, lights up the room from the far side. I know that Gary is planning to do something. Perhaps he is going to use the restroom. Actually, leaving your seat once class has begun is a sin at best, but to do the unthinkable and go outside the premises to the facility, that takes guts.

The other kids can see it, too. Something is about to happen. Somebody is bound to break. This much responsibility is abnormal for children our age with limited intelligence and life experience. What if something bad happens? What if somebody starts bleeding because they get too close to the chain-link gate that separates the corridor from the restrooms and they tear a piece of skin off their hide and they are all alone with no one to see them bleeding and no one to call Mrs. Whitehead for help?

"Everybody stay in their seats!" I declare. Someone needs to be decisive today and, after all, I am the class secretary because I am in charge of the sick kids. So that makes me somebody important, doesn't it? "If you ever want to get another piece of class work to do while you're out sick again, you'll behave, or I'll never deliver you missing work again." That shuts them up real fast.

Until Paul Patton starts busting up. "You actually think I want to be doing your stupid class work while I'm at home sick? Half the time I'm gone it's only because my mom left for work too early and I slept through my alarm. Fool, I'm watching cartoons and eating Captain Crunch for lunch while you're looking in your brown bag to see if that can of orange soda has crushed your egg salad sandwich again. I don't want your boring old work!"

He is so cocky. How dare he say that my organizational skills are nothing but a waste of my time and under-appreciated? How dare he insinuate to the class that people are laughing behind my back as I deliver to their homes the important message of the day, along with the spelling homework that will still need to be turned in on time if they want full credit? And these are the days when I can borrow my brother's bicycle. What about the days when I have to walk to your dumb house to make sure you can keep that stupid "C" you've worked so hard to earn? I have never been so insulted in all of my life. And just when I am about to tell him so, there it is.

That soft-shoe glide across the flooring tile makes us believe Miss Ryan must be a dancer on the weekends, teaching the fox trot to unmarried men so that they can meet a girl and be able to dance at their own wedding. Even in her high heels, she moves as if gravity is reversed and keeps her afloat just an inch above ground. And if she isn't immediately detectable to those of us who know her glide, we can tell by the scent of her heavenly Musk perfume that our Miss Ryan is approaching from the door we dub "the landing strip."

It will take her less time to walk the length of four classrooms than it will for us to jump up from our seat at the back of the room and play tag with the chalkboard at the front, just once, just to know we can get away with it. So, we don't even try. We sit there quietly, with our hands folded. When we hear her sing-song voice say what none of us expects to hear, we are glad we followed her rules.

"Children, I worried all morning while I was stuck behind a truck that turned over in the middle of the highway I take to work, that you might have forgotten some of our rules. I am so proud to know that you have worked really well this morning by yourselves. You are all to be commended for being so responsible. I must have the best fifth grade class in the whole school. Thank you, class. And just for being so well-behaved, I am going to give each of you a dip in the box. Form a quiet line up at my cupboard and you can pick any item you like from our treasure box. You've earned it today."

The smile on Miss Ryan's face makes my heart sing. She makes everything right with the world. And I am so glad that she helps me to feel special in a year when I learn other, not so special, things about myself. For instance, the song "Personality" plays on the radio constantly in 1975. When I ask my mother what the title means, she tells me, "It means that someone is well liked because of who they are. This is why you'll never have any friends, because you don't have a personality." It isn't a slap to the face, but I do manage to increase my count to 24 seconds this time before I surrender to the pain.

Miss Ryan knows more about me than I ever need to tell her. She knows the state report I did on Mississippi was wholly written by my mother, who didn't think I could earn an "A" by myself. Miss Ryan gave out the grades and told us there were only two perfect scores on the state reports this year. Molly Donovan was, of course, one. No surprise there. She has been the smartest kid since kindergarten, and she has the requisite package, curly hair that is wound so tight she makes Pippi Longstocking's wired braids look relaxed. She also has a big mouth of metal, right beneath her big Coke bottle glasses. Plus, we call her beanpole because she is so skinny. So Molly is a given for getting the perfect score on the state paper.

The second name happens to tie Molly's score. In this case, second spot is the biggest honor because the recipient is so surprising. It is me. How astonished I am that I get to go to the front of the room for the first time in my life. I stand up there with Molly, receiving glowing approval from Miss Ryan, while I let the other kids marvel at how smart I am and curiously wonder to themselves how they didn't know that the class secretary could be such a genius. There is a big round of applause for me and Molly, but I largely think it is for me, because we are all so bored with Molly; I think Molly must even be a little bored with herself.

When the time comes for the class to shift to Mrs. Whitehead's room for our Social Studies lesson, Miss Ryan gaily calls across the room and motions for me to come see her. Surely there must be important sick kid business I need to attend to. And I'm sure this is what the other kids think as well. Lickety-split, I am by her side. Directly into my eyes she looks. She is not reading my expression to the question she is about to ask, she is searching my soul for the answer I might craft.

"I want to congratulate you, Vandra, on writing such a perfect paper. You must have worked so very hard on this, because it is by far the best paper you have ever turned in. Vandra, I am so proud of you and you must be so proud of yourself." There she goes, complimenting me and using my name to add the personal touch. I can feel the guilt tears welling up in my throat. I hope they don't make it all the way to the top of my head and start coming out my eyes.

"How long did it take you to do all of this research?" came the first question. I could only reply the honest truth, that I started thinking about Mississippi the day it was assigned to me.

"It is so perfectly articulated, and there is not one error, not even in the footnotes or bibliography. Even Molly had a couple of minor errors, but they weren't important enough to take off any points. But your paper is, indeed, flawless. Flawless." I beam brightly, but only for a minute. I can feel the bile rising in the back of my throat. Push it down, push it down, push it way down, I keep telling myself. Miss Ryan thinks you are a genius. She doesn't know anything. All I can hear in my head is, "Don't say a word and your reputation will be safe. You beat Molly Donovan on the big state report. You'll have new friends and everyone will want to eat lunch with you."

"Did you write this yourself?" Here it is, the final blow.

"I certainly did. I typed the whole thing by myself." I figure that is sly enough to say and that Miss Ryan probably won't catch on that there is a distinction between writing and typing. So, therefore, I am telling the truth, the awful truth.

But Miss Ryan is smarter than me. "You typed the whole report by yourself? Does that mean you had some help writing it?" She is trying to be gentle, but she isn't beating around the bush. The gig is up. My days of having no friends will continue and I will lose bragging rights that I beat Molly Donovan. I will remain a failure. Even worse, kids will realize that my mom had to do my big report for me.

"My mom wrote it, Miss Ryan. I wanted to, but she wanted it to be perfect. So when she got it finished the night before it was due, I sat up until midnight, typing every word, including the bibliography and the footnotes. I worked real hard to make sure I had no typing errors. But when I got up in the morning, my mom was finishing retyping some of the pages that I hadn't checked carefully enough. I really wanted to make you proud Miss Ryan, and I really wanted to do it myself."

And there it is. Twenty-six seconds and I can't hold my bottom lip any longer. The floodgates open and I can feel that warm water gushing down my face. But, through my blurred vision, I can see Miss Ryan's sweet smile sweep across her face. She only has three words for me before she sends me to the restroom. "It's our secret." And with that I am gone. It is a good long wail I have alone in my little bathroom stall. I cherish her for having the courage and the human capacity to see through to my situation.

I will never forget the kindness Miss Ryan has extended to me. What else could she do? I am held hostage by a parent who has very little faith that I can produce my own work, and manipulated me into a losing scenario.

I learn a few things about Mississippi this year. I learn a lot about organizing and taking care of sick kids. But what I learn most in fifth grade is what no other human has ever taught me. Sometimes the experience of our plight is lesson enough. Keeping a close tab on doing the right thing, and following the rules and setting a good example is hard when others want you to do it their way.

I learn that showing kindness to others, and never embarrassing someone who is already in a very embarrassing position, is a gracious way to live your life. Finally, I learn the people who are lucky enough to be on the receiving end of your tender sincerity are likely to never forget your example and will remember to do the same when they meet others in the same predicament.

All of this great profoundness on how to live a decent human life was learned by me at the age of ten, and taught to me by my dear teacher for life, Miss Ryan.

Meeting Kirsten Hansen:
The Last Lesson in Elementary

The summer going into sixth grade, I discover that I have only one real friend. Her name is Kirsten Hansen, but most kids call her other names. She is very blond, and her hair is uncontrollable. It is long and frizzy, but it would be straight and glossy if she knew anything about hair products. All we have for role models are hippies, and they don't seem to have the glossy hair that is advertised on commercials. And the only commercial for hair that we see on television is the one for Faberge Organic Shampoo, where if "you tell two friends, then they'll tell two friends, and so on, and so on, and so on." Great commercial.

I love to watch commercials more than I love to watch some of my favorite shows. The only thing that beats commercials is "The Flintstones," because it is so clever how all the prehistoric animals serve as household tools for doing chores. The pterodactyl uses its choppers to mow the lawn; the monkey sits beneath the sink to eat the garbage that goes down the disposal; the elephant's trunk works like a shower head. It makes me happy to watch, and very few things bring me this kind of joy.

Kirsten and I meet during fifth grade, but we aren't in the same class with Miss Ryan. It is already spring time and all the fifth graders are feeling pretty important in front of all the younger kids. At the same time, we are secretly dreading the idea of being new in middle school next year. I have had a pretty long year of suffering through the embarrassment of not learning my multiplication tables. My dad finally made me a poster sized chart with rows to correspond with the digits 1 to 12 that eventually teach me 12 x 12 is 144. It is another way he comes to my rescue and helps me feel that there is nothing low-performing about me; I just have a different learning style.

So it is on a random Thursday, with two months left to go in school, that Kirsten and I forge a bond. The lunch bell rings and I pull my sack from underneath the classroom sink, where we store our bags for the morning. It feels kind of heavy today, so I am preoccupied by getting to my regular seat on the curb where I can finally peek inside to see what kind of surprise awaits me. It is a sunny day, and I like to sit outdoors, huddled underneath the window sills of our classroom. There is no bench, but the cement curbing is comfortable enough for the 28 minutes I have to enjoy my lunch in peace.

Of course, there are wooden picnic tables, but as usual, the popular kids have reserved seats for their popular friends who are stuck in the cafeteria line. They buy their lunch, resting assured that when they finally do make it outside, there will be a backpack to signal to them that their seat is protected here, and being guarded only for them.

Some days those backpacks are never moved because the lunch line is so long, the kids who buy end up eating off their trays while waiting to pay. It's dumb, really. There would be plenty of room for the curb-eaters if the backpacks weren't in the way. I don't know why someone doesn't tell them this obvious oversight. There are other people who might like to sit at the table, too.

I'd like to sit up there and trade sandwiches with the popular kids. At least, I'd like to tell them one of my jokes and see if they laugh. I bet I could make them laugh. At least one of them might think I am funny. Then, maybe, they would want to hear a second joke, and then maybe they would ask me to come over after school and we could play for awhile before I have to go home.

But no one is saying a word today. Those backpacks just sit there uninterrupted, again.

There is a space on the curb at the end of the row that meets the corner of the building. I am lucky. Some kids have to wrap around the building to eat with their friends, but that means they have to then sit on the ground, which presents two problems: little tiny bits of gravel from the old asphalt get ground up into your butt, which is not comfortable at all; and sometimes there are ant trails near the big garbage can that is stationed around the corner, and ants are always looking for their next snack. So I feel sorry for those kids, but usually they are boys who don't want to be overheard anyway. They are the troublemakers who are planning times to meet at the school where they will run their skateboards atop the roof without getting caught.

I roll back the top three folds of my brown lunch sack and notice that today is no different. There is no name drawn on my bag with little hearts around it. Some days I even scour the inside to see if there is a little love note from mom tucked away somewhere between my pickle and lettuce leaf in my egg salad sandwich. I figure that would be a really good hiding place and a great way to surprise me. I look around and see other kids pulling out notes from the top of their lunch sack, or sometimes they find one attached to a baggie of homemade chocolate chip cookies. I know that some day my note will come and, when it does, I bet it will be bigger than any of the ones those other kids get.

"Oh." A hushed syllable utters through my head. A quiet disappointment swallows me whole when I see that the secret extra special ingredient weighing down today's lunch is just an oversized green apple. I thought for sure it might be one, or maybe two, of those foil wrapped Hostess Ding Dongs. That would be a real treat. I've never even gotten that in my birthday lunches, and boy, don't you know, I have hinted. No such luck. Today's apple is another reminder that there is nothing special for me here. And I secretly wonder why an apple, when everyone in my house knows I hate apples.

I do not like my fruit crunchy. The citrus fruits are the ones that make me happiest. I love the kind of sweet nectarine where the juice just runs down your chin faster than you can catch it with the back of your hand. I love a peach second best. If it weren't for the fur, it would be my number one favorite. I love strawberries, especially the really gigantic ones that still have the big green stems in their tops. Some days, my sister sneaks cherries off the neighbor's tree in their back yard. The limbs grow out along their fence, onto the outside of their property, so she crosses the street and climbs right up to grab handfuls at a time. They taste so good, but I feel guilty eating them stolen.

I later discover that the neighbors told my parents that we should help ourselves because they could never eat the whole harvest, and they figure it's the least they can do to repay my dad for all the salmon he gives them from his regular fishing trips. But my sister is the type who likes to feel as though she's getting away with something, so I don't tell her.

Underneath my big green apple is my mushed sandwich. The tuna fish is squished between my Wonder Bread and has a big dent in the middle where the apple sat. There are some sweet pickle chips in a separate baggie, but the juice seems to have leaked out from underneath the plastic tuck and now I have pickle drippings all over my baggie of carrot sticks that, apparently, didn't even attempt to get closed. That's it. A sandwich and a couple of side baggies. No treats. No drink. No Ho Hos. No sweet nectarine.

In the middle of taking inventory, I feel someone staring at me. I look up, and across from me is that blond girl people call "Horse." She is a big blond girl who likes to ride horses. Some kids are so clever that this is the best they can come up with in the nickname department. They, of course, are the geniuses on campus who like to brute about, intimidating anyone who accidentally looks their way. She just got braces, so all I can see is a mouth full of black metal as she smiles and motions me to come join her on her side of the curb. She doesn't have a seat at the backpack table either.

I sheepishly put the pieces of my lunch back in their sack and toss the apple in the can on the way over to her side of the corridor. "Hi. You're Kirsten, right?"

"Yeah. I always notice you sitting in the exact same spot on the curb that I sit in, only we are on opposite sides. So do you want to eat lunch together? What have you got today?" She is a ray of sunshine.

"Oh, nothing special. I just ate half of my lunch, and today I got some Ho Hos that were out of this world. I still have some carrot sticks. Want some?"

"Nope. I've got carrot sticks, too. You're pretty lucky you got Ho Hos. My mom only lets me eat junk food when I'm not on a diet, and I can't remember the last time I wasn't on a diet."

She seems to be okay with the fact that she doesn't have much of anything special in her lunch either. Her mom packed her a Tupperware of salad from last night's dinner and a little piece of chicken. She had a plum and a baggie full of cherries, which she shares with me. I tell her one of my jokes and she laughs so hard the milk she is drinking from a straw comes out of her nose. It is sort of gross, but it makes me laugh to know that she thinks I am funny. And this is the beginning of how we become friends.

Kirsten and I have a lot in common. We both sort of feel like we are on our own. Even though I have three siblings, they pretty much go to their friends' houses to play, while I am usually in my room organizing my school supplies or attempting to understand my homework. While Kirsten has been mostly a quiet, bookish girl, we both love David Cassidy from the Partridge Family, and we both want to be Marcia Brady on the Brady Bunch. 'How does she get her hair so glossy straight,?' we both wonder. 'She must use Faberge Organic Shampoo,' we agree.

Her house is around the corner from our elementary school, if you start at the top end, where the kindergarten buildings are. My house is across the street, at the bottom end of the school, where our fifth grade building stands. Every day after school her job is to walk her dog. She usually turns the corner from her house and walks through the school grounds, starting at the kindergarten wing, until she comes to the opening in the gate that students use to exit from the fifth grade side. She carefully crosses the street and walks the five houses down on the right before she comes to my house on the corner. I am usually already waiting outside for her to pick me up. I like walking the dog with Kirsten. It gives us a chance to talk about the day at school, and sometimes I tell her stories.

We had been meeting like this for about three weeks when, one day, she didn't show up. I waited and waited, and it seemed like an eternity. I went inside to call her, but no one answered. Pretty soon it was dinner time, and when I called again after supper, there was still no one picking up. I don't know what happened to Kirsten that day, but I know it must have been something pretty bad for her to forget about me.

The next day at school, I look for Kirsten at lunch. She is nowhere. I even look over to scour the picnic tables, just in case she had a backpack reserved for her, but there is no Kirsten there either. Secretly, I'm relieved about that. Today, I decide, I won't wait for her to come to my house. I'll go to her house after school and see if she is sick.

When I get there, her dad is home. He is a nice man. He is tall and blond, and speaks with a German accent. He plays a big piano in their living room, which is filled with artwork in frames all along the walls. I guess he is some big artist and piano player. Her mom is a nurse, and she works the night shift, so she is never home after school.

"Hi, Mr. Hansen. Is Kirsten home sick today?" He greets me with a warm and sincere smile, but I can see his eyes begin to glisten. Is he going to cry? My heart starts rushing a little faster because I wonder if my new friend is okay.

"Come on in, Vandra. Kirsten is a little sad. You see, our dog got off the leash yesterday and got hit by a car. He was pretty badly hurt, so the vet had to put him to sleep. She is just heartbroken and we thought it best that she stay home today. But I'm sure she'd like to see you."

I knocked softly on her door, which was covered with David Cassidy posters. "Kirsten, it's me, Vanny. I came to see how you were doing." I opened the door, and she was trying to grab some Kleenex so that I wouldn't see her cry. "Oh, Kirsten, I'm so sorry. My cat, Cat, got run over by a car last summer, and I know just how you feel. I loved that cat. I wished it could have been his twin, Baby, because Baby really was so dumb. Skipper was a really good dog, and he loved how you took care of him. It'll be okay."

Why was I rambling about Cat? I was trying to make her feel better, but all of a sudden she looked up at me with these teary blue eyes and I started to cry, too. I felt so bad. All she ever wanted was a dog, and now he was gone. Kirsten was an only child, so for her Skipper was like her sibling or her best friend, until I came along. She began to wail, and all we could do was hug.

Two weeks later, Kirsten came by after school with a surprise. Her dad had a new dog waiting for her when she got home, and this puppy was a poodle, just like Skipper, but he wasn't gray, he was all black, so Kirsten named him Pepper. Here she was, outside my door, ready to take this new pup for a walk, so I went along for the great conversation and a chance to play with the spunky guy.

Pepper is the cutest dog, and energetic, more so than Skipper because he is about ten years younger. Every day Kirsten comes by so we can walk him together and, on one particular day, I ask if I can hold his leash.

"My dad told me I am the only one who is allowed to hold his leash because of what happened to Skipper, so I don't think it's a good idea."

"Please. I'll be real careful. We're on the school grounds, so there aren't any cars around. Nothing will happen. I love your dog. I promise to be careful. Please just let me hold his leash just for part of the way. How about only from the kindergarten building to the third grade building? What do you say? Come on. Please," I begged. Her dog is so cute, I just have to see what it feels like to hold his leash and walk him by myself. I wish I had a dog. I've been asking for one since I was seven, but no such luck.

Kirsten looks at me with these pleading eyes that speak words she never has to utter. "Only for the length of two buildings and you have to stay right next to me, don't get ahead, and finally, you have to wrap the leash around your wrist so Pepper doesn't fly off into a run. Keep him close, and promise me you won't let go." Her trusting voice deserves all of the calming reassurance I can offer back. I promise everything she asks, and she turns over the leash.

As if on cue, Pepper realizes there is a changing of the guard and uses this fleeting opportunity to pull a fast one. He charges into a sprint faster than any Olympian at the sound of the starting gun and he is off.

An unmerciful cry comes from Kirsten that is certainly heard by families far outside of the neighboring homes within blocks of the school. "Vanny!" she screams in slow motion with a bloodcurdling cringe. "Get Pepper!"

Before she even comprehends that the trade-off is a bust, I am in motion, hightailing after a dog who is running at a feverish pace, as any pup with newfound freedom would trek. I scream behind Pepper calling his name as if to say, "Stay! Come! Sit!" all in one failed attempt. There is only the lingering sound that echoes throughout the school corridor, "P-e-p-p-e-r-r-r-r-r-r!"

I am breathing hard. My heart hurts. I am not fat, but I am not a fan of P.E., and I am always last to be picked for any team sport. And I am not invited to participate when the fifth graders sign up to play softball against the teachers on the last day of school. So, running after this spirited dog is taking all the wind out of me. Suddenly, I clumsily cross a rock the size of a mere kiwi, and it downs me. I cannot lose my momentum now. Pepper is just turning the corner. After he discovers that open gate, beyond the fifth grade building, he'll be heading straight out into oncoming traffic.

"Oh, God, please let me catch him before Kirsten loses another dog," I silently prayed.

The rattling and clanking of the chain that leads to the leather loop of the handle on his leash is whipping alongside me. Somewhere within my forward tumbling from tripping over that rock and rolling in fast motion along the cement rampway of building five, my index finger threads that loop and I clasp my hand so hard around the leather gripping that I can hear Pepper give a little yelp as he is stopped dead in his tracks and flung back on his hind quarters from the greatest chase of his little life. I've got him. I am bloody and I am shaking and I am hurt, but I've got him.

It is the single greatest achievement of my life. I have never won anything before this moment. I have never been lucky. I have never found a quarter lying in the gutter. But today, my prayer is answered and I got him. I am so unclear as to how I could have possibly managed to tangle my finger through the loop that was dodging and whipping past me, but here, I have it. Pepper is not running anymore, and Kirsten is crying tears of joy. I am crying too, because my ankle really hurts, and I am so relieved that I didn't kill my friend's new dog. After this heroic action, Kirsten knows I will do anything for her and her dog, and we are for sure best friends forever now. She continues to come to my house every day for our walk. And I only go along for the company and never ask to hold Pepper's leash again.

The last month of school is upon us and there are three parting events fifth graders will be leading. First, there is the teacher versus student softball game, which I know was reserved only for the popular kids who sit regularly at the backpack table. Then, there will be the Last Day Dance, where we will all meet at the Rec. Center for swimming, disco dancing and hot dogs.

I have a huge crush on Mark Jines, but I think he's been avoiding me ever since that day of tag out on the playground when I accidentally made him run into a steel pole. He was trying to back up from me, and when he sprang right around, charging toward his great escape, BAM!, he smacked straight into the iron pole that supports the cage around the school generator. He went blind for three days. I thought I killed him, the way he laid on the ground motionless. He's been a little gun shy around me ever since, but at least he got his eyesight back. The doctor said it was only temporary blindness. I tried to warn him, but he was moving so fast there wasn't enough time. So disco dancing with him is probably out of the question.

Finally, there is the fifth grade Talent Show that we put on as an assembly for the whole school to come and watch. Kirsten and I look at each other when we hear the announcement and communicate silently to one another that this is where we will have our most fun in fifth grade. So we meet after school to plan a fabulous act. Could either of us sing? No. Could we act? No. What are some of our competitors doing?

"All I know is that Maureen Stafford and Molly Donovan and the rest of the backpack table party are singing their own made-up lyrics to "Love Will Keep Us Together," I try to say with more disdain than envy. Those girls will do anything to remind people they are the coolest. Captain and Tennille's single smash hit of the 1970s is on the radio every forty-five minutes. I know because I am always trying to call in and win some kind of prize when it is being played. But I am never fast enough because my family has a rotary dial telephone, not one of those new touch-tone phones. So I never win.

"They would pick the most popular song to sing. What are they changing the lyrics to?" Kirsten was trying to formulate a counter attack plan and needed more details.

"All I know is that they changed the title to be "Hate Will Keep Us Apart," and every time they go to the girls' bathroom together, they come out humming and giggling like they have this groovy routine down. I bet you they win." Already I'm feeling a little defeated.

As we sit listening to music, there it is, my other favorite song, coming on the radio. I start singing along with the upbeat tempo, "…You come on like a dream, peaches and cream, lips like strawberry wine. You're sixteen, you're beautiful, and you're mine."

We sit up, jump off the bed, and say together as if we are one mind, "Let's do this song!"

So, we concoct this whole idea that will be so cool Maureen Stafford and Molly Donovan will be so jealous they didn't think of it first.

"We'll make poodle skirts, since the song is sort of old-fashioned sounding. We'll get little scarves to tie around our necks, and we'll do a little partner dance routine where we have to hold hands and swing each other around."

I want to be the girl. Kirsten has to do the boy parts.

"Oh, it'll be so much fun, and then people will see how cool we really are."

We sign up the next day to register our dance act. And for the following two weeks, we practice every day after school in Kirsten's room. Our skirts are coming along, and we find some scarves to match. And, finally, the big day arrives. Our act follows Maureen Stafford and Molly Donovan. We patiently sit in the audience while they all take their places on our mock stage. The familiar beat booms through the library's loudspeakers and all the kids start shoulder dancing in their floor seats.

"*Hate. Hate will keep us apart… Think of me baby never …* blah, blah, blah." They are singing it loud and proud. They have on groovy leather jackets with dark sunglasses. They are rocking out and the kids are eating it up. They get the biggest standing cheer of the talent show so far. I look around the room, and I see a lot of the teachers smiling and tapping their feet and clapping at the end, too. Hmmmm. We're next.

"Kirsten, we've got to be really good to beat them. They think they've already won. Just look at them squealing on the sidelines, huddled in a group hug, like football players calling their next play." All Kirsten can do is to tell me we're as ready as we're ever going to be. We wait for our names to be called.

Our music begins to play and we come out from our opposite corners. We clasp hands and bounce together, then pull apart, just as we rehearsed. We do some twirls, and some under the arm walk-throughs and more twirls. We want to show that our poodle skirts really can spin. Kirsten tried to flip me around her waist in rehearsals, but she couldn't do it without dropping me on the floor, after which we would start in on hysterical convulsions of laughter as if there had never been anything funnier than me landing on my head, just like the day before.

The last part of our routine runs short, and as our music keeps playing, we have to ad-lib our dance moves. The only step we really know is the bridge move, where we come together and then pull apart, so we just keep doing this over and over again for the last minute of the song. Finally, and thankfully, it ends. I guess we weren't better than the "Hate Will Keep Us Apart" group, but at least we got out there and did our best. And we sure had fun practicing every day after school. So what if our applause wasn't as loud as the Maureen and Molly routine. We sure did have on cute skirts. I may even wear mine to school tomorrow.

Promotion comes and goes and the summer remains filled with the days of dog walking for me and Kirsten. When my birthday comes, Kirsten gives me the most beautiful necklace; it is a flat silhouette of an angel in eighteen carat gold, and it has my name and birth date inscribed in cursive. I am so touched. I have never been given anything so fancy before. This is how I know Kirsten really loves me. And what I did to save her dog is nothing compared to what Kirsten does to save me in sixth grade.

.

Sixth Grade with Mr. Bailey

It is two weeks before sixth grade starts. I am getting a little nervous about what it will be like to go to school with big kids. I got pretty used to being the oldest, and one of the tallest kids in my elementary. I hear we will be getting bused to a school downtown about twenty minutes away, and I wonder why I can't go to the school two miles away where some of the really smart kids are attending. I guess there is a list determined by where you live and if you are on one side of the road you can choose your school; if you're on the other side of the road, like I am, you are getting bused downtown. Still, two weeks away is fourteen days for me to play.

My mom says that I can finally have a dog and she is calling it my late birthday present. My parents have some old friends who live pretty far away, in Sacramento, and their dog just had puppies. My mom has reserved a little white puppy for my sister, and its sister, who is black, will be for me. I am so excited to tell Kirsten that we will both have little black dogs. But I won't name mine Pepper because she already has that name for her dog. I'll probably call mine Midnight, or maybe I'll just have to name it when I see it. Maybe it won't look like a Midnight. Maybe it will look like an Ash. My sister is going along for the ride. I wish I could go, too, but I have a baby-sitting job for five hours.

Mrs. Milligan pays me a quarter a kid, and she has four kids, so that's pretty good money for me. Sometimes, though, I think she really takes advantage of my willingness to work hard. There is usually a load of dishes for me to do in the kitchen sink, and it's a double-wide sink, so that's a lot of dishes. I can tell that some of those dishes have been sitting all week, waiting for me, because there is dried cereal stuck to the side of the bowls and I have to soak them for a long time. I wish the Milligan's had a dishwasher; it'd make my job so much easier. When I'm done in the kitchen, I fold the clothes of four children under the age of six.

But, the absolute worst part of the job is cleaning the dirty diapers. She leaves a paint stick for me, perched inside the toilet bowl, where the doody diapers are soaking. I have to swirl the nappies, as she calls them, around, swishing them until they are emptied of the load that little Paul has put into them. When they are nearly white, I wring them out before putting them in the laundry machine. I detest this part of the job. But then I have to remind myself, I am getting paid $1 an hour, and that's pretty good money for any eleven year old. I can buy at least four different Big Hunk bars at the Five and Dime store, where all my favorite candy is under ten cents, and still manage to save half my money.

I have been home for about two hours at the end of this long day when I hear the station wagon pulling into the driveway. I run eagerly through the front door to meet my parents at the car so I can carry in my new puppy. Happy day, happy day.

I knew I would finally get a dog if I was just patient. I made a long list of the reasons why I am responsible enough to care for a dog and to walk it with Kirsten, and to love it, and to feed it, and to clean up after it. My dad thought it was a great list, and my mom went along with it when she found out there would be two dogs available.

My sister slinks from the car first, carrying her little blond furball in a tiny baby blanket. I have to peek at it while it is sleeping. I hope mine is awake so we can play. I ask my sister what she is naming her dog and she says, "Marshmallow. But mom says we can call it Marlo for short. I'm taking her in the house now." And off she went.

I look in the back seat for another little bundle, but there isn't even a blanket in sight. I ask my dad where the other dog is. He gives me a familiar look that makes my heart hurt before I fully know what is happening.

My mother begins, "You know, we had planned to get two dogs, but the more I thought about it, the more I decided it might just be too much for us to have more than one pet right now. So we got the dog for your sister, and I'm sure we will all enjoy Marlo together." It is so matter of fact. So final. So cruel.

"You told me I could have a dog because I was so responsible. I'm the older child. Why don't I get to have a dog first? You even told me my dog was already picked out. Sabrina's never home. Who's going to pick up after Marlo? I can't believe this. I told Kirsten I'd be able to walk my dog with her dog every day."

All of my logic falls on deaf ears. The decision is made and my mother doesn't have anything more to say on the subject. Nothing is offered to make me feel better, except for that knowing glance my father shoots me as if to say, "I feel your pain, honey. I've lived with her longer than you, and I feel your heartache." That look just makes me sadder.

The first day of school comes on the Tuesday after Labor Day. I wear my new black Ditto pants, the kind that have a seam that runs like an upside-down horseshoe across the backside and down the back pant legs. I also wear the matching black T-shirt that is trimmed in a soft yellow cuff around the capped sleeves and the neckline. With my olive skin and long dark hair, it's a flattering look that helps me blend into the background. I don't like to wear "notice me" colors, like some of the other girls do. I just want to go to school, make friends, and come home to a happy house, even though I don't have a dog.

Kirsten meets me at the bus stop, which is in front of the kinder-garten building at my old elementary. She lives about three houses away from where the bus pulls up. She practically waits until she hears the diesel engines of the bus rounding the corner before she decides to grab her lunch and walk out the door. I have to get up early and usually end up waiting in line for about ten minutes so that I am not going to get a seat last on the bus. It's very embarrassing, I hear, to have to ask kids to move their backpack so you can sit with them on their bench seat.

There are a lot of really big kids waiting at the bus stop and I try not to look at any of them. They are talking really loudly and pushing each other around. They don't care that they keep knocking into us sixth graders; we might as well be invisible. The bus comes, Kirsten joins me and we are off to our very first day of middle school. Hurrah.

Our bus ride to the school is an adventure. We drive to a part of town I've never been to before. There is a high school right across the street and I see a lot of scary kids smoking outside and acting real cool. I know this will not be the high school I attend because it is too far away from where I live. My future high school is really pretty, with lots of trees around it, and it is near the shopping mall. That's how I know I won't be going to the high school I am sneaking peeks at now.

We are greeted by Dr. William Kramer, the Principal, and his Vice Principal, Mr. Russell Bailey. They give us a speech about the rules of the school and the lunchtime procedures and how violence will not be tolerated. No vandalism. No swearing. No ditching classes. They will not hesitate to suspend anyone caught doing any of these things. "Now, welcome to Stanyan Middle School. Have a great day."

Dr. Kramer scares me because he doesn't talk much. It is almost as if he is too powerful to interact with children who have less intelligence than he. However, Mr. Bailey is even more frightening because he actually looks like a creature from outer space. He has a big shiny dome with some graying hair that is trimmed short from ear to ear. His eyes seem to always be squinting behind his rose colored spectacles. He rarely smiles, and the kids hate him. They call him mean names and write bad words next to graffiti illustrations of him on the bathroom walls. I sort of feel sorry for Mr. Bailey because he has no idea how many kids think he's useless. But this is just what I've heard today. I come to find out soon enough that Mr. Bailey can be useful for many things.

By the end of my first month in sixth grade, I am making friends with my teachers and signing up to be an office assistant. I was, after all, a very top-notch secretary for Miss Ryan, so I want to further my experience in the arena of paper shuffling, stapling, filing and organizing whatever the front office secretaries deem worthy of delegating. It is quite a big opportunity for a sixth grader to work in the front office. Anyone who gets to work near Mrs. Crandall's desk usually sees a lot of top secret stuff. She is Head Secretary, and the first person you see when you walk in. Sometimes suspended kids have to sit with Mrs. Crandall until the principal is available. We get to hear the whole story of why they got kicked out of class. We also get the first glance at the upcoming social activities for the month. There is always some kind of drama unfolding at our dances. I love to see which eighth grade couples are breaking up and making up.

Finally, being an office assistant sometimes requires errands being run to other classrooms. On one such occasion, I am asked to drop a message for a student in one of the eighth grade classes. I am wearing my cute Dittos and, evidently, a couple of the eighth grade boys notice me. Completely unaware of all this attention, I have stirred up the eighth grade girls who decide I am trying to steal their boyfriends. It takes about a week for them to formulate a club of torturers who are willing to follow me through the halls at lunchtime to accost me and scare me out of my wits.

"Oooooh, look at her wiggle with that walk," they hiss at me. "She thinks she is hot stuff all right. Just look at her with those clothes that she thinks make her look so cute," they continue. "You think you can take our boyfriends, but it's never gonna happen. When we get done with you, no guy is ever gonna want to look at you again. We're gonna pull your hair out in clumps until you go bald. And then we're gonna bust your mouth until you lose a couple of your front teeth. You won't be such hot stuff then, will you?"

It happens. It only takes fourteen seconds this time before the tears erupt in me and my voice starts to crack. I don't know where Kirsten is, and all of the yard duty seem to be suspending kids who are playing dodge ball too brutally somewhere on the playground. I was just minding my own business, trying to find my way to the library, since I don't have a lunch today.

"I'm not bothering you. Why can't you just leave me alone?" is all I can say in a most timid voice. I want them to think they have scared me enough so they will just leave me alone. I want them to think I have learned whatever lesson they are trying to teach me. I realize it must be, "Never smile when I walk into an eighth grade classroom because a boy might think I like him. Better yet, never go into an eighth grade classroom unless I am in the eighth grade."

They come closer and begin to huddle around me. "What did you say, girl? I thought I heard you call me a wench. Did you guys hear her call me a wench? You are as stupid as you look." Suddenly, from the back, I feel someone push me so hard it knocks the wind out of me as I fall to the ground. I try not to get my hands all cut up from the loose gravel on the asphalt, but I am crying and feeling humiliated. Isn't anybody going to come to my rescue?

I look up at them with tears streaming down my face, and they are laughing at me. I look around to see if any adults are coming, and I only see Kirsten. She is standing in a far corner of the corridor with the saddest look on her face like she wants to help but she doesn't know how to get me out of here without them coming after her, too.

The lunch bell rings. I am saved. All of the teachers who were eating in their rooms kick open their doors and the crowd scatters. I am getting up from the ground when one teacher I don't know asks if I am okay. He couldn't tell if I had tripped. I know the eighth grade girls are watching me from around the corner, so I only say I fell over a rock and that I am fine.

Kirsten comes running to me with tears in her eyes. "I am so sorry I couldn't help. It happened so fast, I didn't know if I should try to find any yard duties. They all seemed so far away and I didn't want those girls to beat you up. Some of those girls ride the bus with us. What are we going to do?"

This just makes me feel worse. I had forgotten that they rode to our neighborhood. "I think they know they'll get in big trouble from the bus driver if they do anything on the bus. Let's just stick together." I try to sound confident, but I really am not feeling very well. I want to go lie down in the office and skip sixth period, but I don't. Kirsten and I go to class, and I try to focus on Spanish.

Someone passes me a note that says, "Warning: you're going to get beat up by Helen Norman after school today. Good Luck." I guess I should be happy that someone cares enough to warn me of my impending doom three hours before my uncertain fate. My lip is puffing in and out and I don't know how to control it. It seems to be tugging on my eyelids, because they begin to fill with tears. I try to cover my face with my long hair, leaning downward, face planted in my book. I pretend to be engrossed in this boring paragraph, which I have read eighteen times and still don't know what it means. How could I be so unpopular at the beginning of my middle school career?

The school bell rings and everyone is scrambling to catch their bus. No one is looking at me, so I figure it's just a rumor. Kirsten and I board our regular seats together and barely speak for the twenty minute ride home. No one is saying mean things to me. I am feeling much better now that we are almost at my stop. It's the last one on the route, and the bus is pretty empty. Kirsten and I walk off together and I promise to call her when I get home. I walk through the hallowed halls of my former elementary, starting with the kindergarten building, and move down the ramp toward the fifth grade hall until I see the open gate that leads me across the street to my corner house. I am home. I am safe. I am happy.

"Hello? Mom, where are you?" I anxiously call out. Before I get to the middle of our entry hall, she greets me with a warm hello. It's a good day to get a warm hello.

"How was your day today, child?" She sounds interested. I tell her nothing really went on except I got to help in the office again today. When the normal after-school rush seems to calm itself from brothers coming home looking for snacks, sister swishing in to call friends for play dates that whisk her out again within five minutes, there is a sound outside the front door that beckons me to the street.

"Toot, toot. Toot, toot," sounds the horn, followed by the frenzy of giggling girls in the back seat. "Oh, Vandra," my name is sung, "we wanted to apologize for what happened today," is the way it begins.

My spirit lifts for a moment and I am ready to say, "Oh, it's okay. Let's just forget it and be friends," but they aren't finished with the message.

"We wanted to, but instead we brought you a gift. We think you left it at school." With this, an egg comes flying at me and hits my shoulder before it slams up against the glossy black trim of the front shutters on our bay window. I am mortified, and terrorized. These girls have the nerve to drive up to my house and egg me right in front of everybody, even though nobody was around to see it happen. "Chicken," they chirp and holler as they speed off, screeching tires behind them. I can hear their devilish howls from far around the corner their older sister twists behind, breaking all the safety speed laws of our neighborhood.

For two weeks, I endure the same fate each day at school with the idealistic hope that somehow it will end as mysteriously as it began. Each day, I try to have someone walk with me from fourth period to lunch. Most days I am lucky, but Thursday ends my streak and I am trapped by a gang of bullies who surround me in the sixth grade wing once again. I am open bait. There is never any yard supervision nearby when you need it. But this time Kirsten stands firmly by my side. "Leave her alone," she says with a mighty voice that cracks only subtly enough for me to detect that she is nervous too.

"Get out of the way, you stupid vanilla wafer. Were you born albino? Because you need to get into the sun, white girl." We are both fair game now, but it does feel good to have company.

"You sure don't know how to take a hint. We thought you would have learned by now that you shouldn't be looking at our boyfriends. Maybe this'll remind you that you're gonna be ugly and bald by the time we get through with you."

There are at least thirteen girls swirling around me. The ugliest ones snarl at me through mouths full of metal that remind me of the rows of staple bars I am always refilling in the office. I know at least half of these girls really have no interest in harming me, but they are trying to be cool and go along with Helen Norman, their vicious leader.

Someone yanks on my hair, hard, pulling at it from behind. While I am being held motionless, Helen slaps my face. She thinks I've never been slapped before and that I should look a lot more surprised or hurt than I do. I am angry on the inside, and every slap stings, but this is something that is not unfamiliar to me. My mother prides herself on having the quickest backhand in the West.

This lack of emotional registry only inspires her to smack me a few more times, even harder, as if I didn't really feel her weighty blows the first time around. By now, there are catcalls heard through all the wings: "Girl fight, girl fight, sixth grade hall." It is over in a flash as soon as everyone hears the lunch bell ring. Again, no one says a word, and I go to the girls' bathroom with Kirsten, crying my eyes out.

"You have to tell somebody about this. Go get Mr. Bailey. He'll put a stop to this. You can't keep running home everyday hoping they won't catch you," Kirsten pleads.

I am so afraid of every one of the eighth graders ganging up on me. Right now, it's pretty bad with thirteen girls. But they all have friends, and I don't want the entire student body to be hassling me. But, of course, I am crying too hard to share any of these thoughts. "It's going to stop, I know it. They've done all they can do. If it happens one more time, I'll tell my mom." I sound convincing, even to me.

The bus ride home is quiet. Kirsten and I form an emergency plan. If it looks like Helen Norman and Sara Swanson are getting off the bus first and waiting for me to step off last, then I am supposed to run around the corner to Kirsten's house because she has the closest getaway. Today, we need the plan to work.

The bus driver pulls to my stop and sees a rush of girls heading out the door and just hovering around the metal pole that says "Bus Stop." He is real smart and gets a sense that everything might not be okay by the way they are peering through the windows awaiting my departure. "Are you going to be all right if I let you off here?" he pretends he can help me out of this harrowing situation.

"Yeah. I'm going to my friend's house right around the corner. But thanks, I'll be fine," I muster up. I try not to look at the predators just loitering casually. I wrap my arms tightly around my school books so they don't get ripped from my grip. I do have school work to do tonight and I would like to be able to get it done with the aid of my books intact. I step onto the curb and sense that the crowd has grown bigger. Someone slaps my head up against the metal pole as the bus pulls away. I can hear a ringing in my ear where it hits the steel, but I still have all my teeth, and if I throw down my books I can run faster. On the rebound from the pole banging I hear Kirsten scream, "Run, Vanny. Run to my house, fast as you can!"

It's all in slow motion, but the books are behind me, some even land in the gutter. I'm sure the pages are being torn out of them right now, while people are probably stomping on the gingham fabric covers I so carefully cut out and stitched myself. It's bad enough they're abusing me, but now my matching books and folders are being muddied and mocked.

I make it to Kirsten's house in record time and hide behind the bushes so no one can see me if they come looking. Kirsten shows up just a few minutes later, and we both agree that today I need to tell my mom that I am being harassed. "Call me after you talk to your mom and tell me everything she says." I promise I will.

After stalling over some Oreo cookies and milk at Kirsten's, just to give Helen Norman and Sara Swanson enough time to think I am not ever coming out again, I walk home the four long blocks between us in about ten minutes. "Mom, where are you? I'm home from school," I call through the door.

There she is, coming from her bedroom down the hallway, not necessarily to greet me, but, coincidentally, I am there on her way to the kitchen. "How was your day, dear?" she inquires sincerely.

"Not very good. Can we talk about it in the living room?" This is our serious room that is usually reserved only for fancy guests. But some days, when it is the only clean room in the house, this is where we can gather to read or chat with anyone who is willing to listen. Today, it is my turn to tell my mom what has been happening, really happening, at school. I begin at the beginning and end with the hair pulling and head pole slamming from just twenty minutes ago.

"These girls are scaring me and they are always looking to beat me up. I am afraid to tell anyone at school because I think it will make things worse. Everyone will find out that I'm a squealer and then there will be more people who hate me." The tears begin to gush. "I hate school, and I am miserable, and Kirsten is my only friend."

I can't stop the geyser that is free-flowing now. And then the moment comes. I think I might have gone numb for a minute. Did I hear her? What did she just say? I rewind instant replay in my head and the image and the wording repeats slowly again. "Well, dear, sometimes this is just part of life, and growing up is expected to be difficult. This, too, shall pass."

This is what I get? "This, too, shall pass?" After pouring my heart out, after concealing this pain for weeks, this is all the comfort I am allotted? I might as well drown my sorrows alone in my room. At least there I can hold onto Giraffey, my stuffed giraffe, who used to feel life-sized when I was eight years old. Now he only comes up to my knees.

I must have cried myself to sleep because I am awakened by my dad's gentle forehead kiss as he pats my head to say goodnight. He is finally home from his business trip, and it is so unlike me to not be standing in the driveway for the hour preceding his anticipated arrival, he knows something is wrong and asks accordingly.

I blubber to him the story I relayed to mom earlier, and this is the only reply I got. "I'm going to put a stop to this right now. You will never have to experience another moment of fear from these girls. What they are doing is illegal and it is called harassment. It doesn't matter that they are children. I will take care of this tonight. Let me get on the phone." It was the only reply I needed.

My dad called Officer Blum, our local neighborhood sheriff, to report the incidents. He went to pay a visit to Helen Norman's father and Sara Swanson's dad. He didn't know them, but he believed any father would want to know how his daughter is treating other people. It's about how children represent their families, and he couldn't imagine these men would be proud of the way their daughters were heralding the family name. The next day, my dad met with Vice Principal Bailey, and Mr. Bailey put an end to my troubles.

Mr. Bailey becomes my personal escort to lunch, and to sixth period after lunch. He makes sure there are at least two yard duties assigned to the sixth grade wing. He calls in the kids who I said had witnessed the many assaults at school and makes them believe that if they lie to him, they will be in worse trouble for covering it up and it will be on their permanent record. In general, we are all afraid of what will be on our permanent record, so that's always a pretty good way of getting kids to talk.

Mr. Bailey gets Helen Norman and Sara Swanson to apologize to me in front of him and to write my parents a letter of apology for throwing eggs at me and our house. He also makes them do community service at our school. They have to clean graffiti off all the bathroom walls, including the boys' bathroom, where it smells like pee, even from the outside when you walk by the door. They do bathroom duty for two and a half weeks, the same amount of time they had been harassing me.

Helen Norman and Sara Swanson are banned from going to any Sadie Hawkins activities or the upcoming Halloween dance for eighth graders only. They have to sit in the office and write a report on what harassment really means, how to recognize it, and how to protect those who are being harassed. It has to be twenty pages in length, and when it is done they can rejoin student body activities.

It doesn't matter to Mr. Bailey how many weeks or months this takes. For every school activity on the calendar, he has two chairs in his office with their names on it. They will write while their friends are enjoying themselves at assemblies, talent shows and dances. And if they still don't have it done by the time promotion comes in June, then they will not be walking across the stage with their class; their diploma will be mailed.

Mr. Bailey is serious. He is not about to let a sixth grader be harassed on his watch. He feels pretty bad that it has gone on without his knowledge for two-and-a-half weeks, so he really makes it up to me. He gives me five "Free Item" cards for the student snack shack. I split a Coke or Sprite with Kirsten every day of the week.

Helen Norman's dad is so embarrassed by her behavior that her family moves over Christmas vacation. Sara Swanson gets a perm that turns out really badly and she has to wear a head scarf for three months. Mr. Bailey becomes my best friend and I never talk badly behind his back to other kids who don't like him. I visit with him in his office some days during lunch and he always makes time for me.

Between Kirsten and Mr. Bailey, I survive sixth grade. Of course, my dad is the real hero. But as far as knowing who all the players were who really made the situation die, my dad knew it was Mr. Bailey. I think they had a secret meeting and agreed that my dad would protect me on the home front and Mr. Bailey would take care of me at school.

Mr. Bailey and I remain friends through my years at Stanyan. I never forget how he helped me. And in two years, when other kids will walk across our stage at promotion to shake only Dr. Kramer's hand as they greedily grab their diplomas from Mr. Bailey, I will still remember my experience with him in the sixth grade. When the last name of the school roster is finally called, I rise from my chair and walk slowly across the stage. Before Mr. Bailey can hand me my diploma, I reach for his hand and shake it hard. I don't let go until I can see the tears welling up in his eyes. I will be the only one who doesn't ignore him on the stage this day.

In this year of sixth grade I learn that heroes don't always wear capes. Behind those beady little eyes, there is a warmth in Mr. Bailey that not too many kids were lucky enough to unmask. He probably has kids of his own. And it probably makes him cry when he thinks about the idea of any one of them getting beat up every day like I did.

I learn that justice does prevail, if you can involve people who understand the rules of law. I learn that bullies are really only weaklings when they have to face someone more powerful than themselves.

I learn that true friends will stand with you to face your fear together. I learn that escape routes and backup plans are necessary to avoid evil trappings.

I learn that my dad is a man of action. There is no time like the present to handle a problem. Make some noise. Get in front of people. Be heard. Be reasonable, be firm, be fearless. This is the only way to resolve the matter.

I also learn that sometimes people you count on will let you down. Keep moving in forward motion. Find another answer. And when that happens, the words "This, too, shall pass" won't sound so helpless.

Seventh Grade with Mr. Koker

Chapter 9

In the year we discover there are harder drugs out there than regular old marijuana, we end up with a new teacher at school, coincidentally named Mr. Koker. He is young, and seems like someone who might actually know something about life outside of school. He is immediately popular, despite his indifference to making friends with twelve-year olds. He likes to wear a tweed jacket with elbow patches made of suede, the color of butterscotch. Clearly, he does not match. Mr. Koker does not realize that his sea blue shirt contrasts gravely with his professor-like tweed browns, and especially with the butterscotch elbows.

He is our science teacher now. We drove Mrs. Moore crazy. I didn't have much to do with her departure, but I probably didn't make matters any easier for her. She was just not fit to be in the classroom with a bunch of wild kids. We could never hear her voice over all the noise, and she could only hold our attention for the length of time it took us to take a good long gasp at what she chose to wear to school that day.

While her housecoat was probably left in the comforts of her home, it was her granny nightgown attire that made us believe she was not cut out for middle school. She wore a lot of soft colored dresses, with small bunches of floral prints that cascaded around evenly throughout the pattern. Her dresses always tied loosely at the neckline and her hem never came above her mid calf. I am sure she wore two slips because those dresses were not made of anything but cotton, the washable kind that begins to thin after years of tumbling in the dryer. She gifted us with a display of muu muus for two months before she decided to take a leave of absence.

While Mr. Koker possesses questionable taste in his jacket patches, at least he is fully dressed and looks the part of someone who might actually command a little respect. By the time he starts his science class, the tweed jacket comes off and a long white lab coat is donned while he teaches us about the proper technique in using a microscope and analyzing stems of plants.

I secretly really like Mr. Koker. I don't want people to think I have a dumb schoolgirl crush, so I don't tell a soul. Also, Mr. Koker apparently has a girlfriend. He's twenty seven, and they have been dating for five years. They met in college at University of California at Davis. He was a biology major and she was in veterinary science. I wonder if they're getting married. Evidently, other girls are wondering the same thing because somebody has already done their homework on Mr. Koker.

I feel much more relaxed about school this year, now that those awful eighth grade girls are out of my life. Kirsten Hansen moved away. Her dad got a job in Santa Barbara at an art gallery, and we don't keep in touch anymore. I will always have the angel necklace Kirsten gave me for my birthday, and I will always have the memory that there was one friend in my life who was willing to do anything for me. She will always be my angel.

There is another girl who seems real popular already. She is new at Stanyan, and if it doesn't make me sound like a weirdo, I think she is beautiful. She has silky blond hair that falls past her shoulders. The color reminds me of vanilla pudding. It is a really soft yellow, but almost white. She has a naturally olive complexion, so she radiates. I wonder if I could ever be friends with someone so pretty. Everyone is already talking about her because she just moved here from San Diego. Her family lives in the rich part of town and she is adopted. Hold on. She is adopted? Wow! We already have one thing in common. Maybe my chances for making friends with her will be better than I thought.

It turns out that Leslie Hinton and I have a lot more in common than just our biological mysteries to unfold. We have social studies together and we share the same sense of humor; what's even stranger is that we share the same unique seal bark kind of laughter when someone really gets us into a hysterical frenzy. Even though people seem annoyed at the loud noises we make through snorts and giggles, we cannot control ourselves and, frequently, we have tears running out of our eyes until we can hardly breathe. It feels so good to laugh with someone. She likes my jokes and I like to listen to her gut-wrenching guffaws. Leslie and I become fast friends, and everything is right with the world.

Mr. Koker decides that what our school really needs is a school newspaper. He has dabbled in journalism throughout his college career and fancies himself a bit of a writer. With this grand idea, and his willingness to head Journalism as an elective class during winter semester, he gets the go-ahead from the administration and announces it to all of his classes. We, of course, get first pick at signing up.

"Vandra, I hope you are planning to join the newspaper. You have a great way of organizing your assignments, and your summary writing is very strong. I think you will make a great contribution to our staff," went the praise from Mr. Koker, my beloved teacher. Those butterscotch patches are beginning to grow on me and don't look as bad as they did the first week of school.

"Wow, thanks Mr. Koker. If you think I can do it, I'd love to sign up. There will probably be a lot of eighth-graders who will want to join. Do you really think there will be enough room for us seventh-graders?" I am feeling my way around here, seeing how willing he is to feed me just one more compliment to live off of for the rest of the week.

Like a good teacher, he doesn't disappoint. With a knowing glance, and a super friendly smile, he gives me the words of encouragement that had never been uttered before. "You are a really good writer, and you work tremendously hard. I think, with your organizational skills, you could really be in charge of one of the newspaper feature departments, eventually. Go for it!"

And with that, I am ready to try anything. I will not disappoint Mr. Koker. I will become the best writer in the whole student body. With encouragement like this, how can I fail? I can't wait to find Leslie to tell her my news, and I can't wait to have Bus #46 drop me off six blocks from home so I can run the rest of the way to tell my mom. She'll be proud of this, for sure.

Leslie is waiting for me by my locker after school. It begins our end of the day ritual. First, we meet at our lockers to say goodbye. Then, we call each other in an hour to see if we understand our homework, or are actually doing our homework, or, more accurately, to talk about Joshua Fields, the biggest heartthrob in the seventh grade, and maybe the whole school. Now he's exciting, not like the other boys my age.

Josh is probably the only boy under thirteen years old who has already been lifting weights for three years. He has shoulders on him that make him swagger when he walks. He also reads the newspaper. The newspaper! What kid our age is interested in world events? Hunky Josh Fields, that's who. He wants to be somebody important when he grows up, if he doesn't become a professional baseball player. He even told me once that he drinks coffee with his dad in the morning before school, after lifting. His hazel eyes make him Stanyan's biggest dreamboat. He's even handsome with his braces, which happen to hide most of his super white teeth.

"You'll never guess what." I am practically spilling over my words with excited hand gestures that wave wildly, banging clumsily against my locker. "Mr. Koker practically told me I should for sure sign up for Journalism because he is going to put me in charge of one of the departments, ahead of any of the eighth graders, because he thinks my writing and my organizational skills are so good," I blurt out in one long stream of connected syllables.

Before Leslie has a chance to give any facial signs of recognition from my prattling, I continue. "You know, Miss Ryan thought the same thing, the very same thing. In fact, she was the one who first told me that I should be in charge of the sick kids because I was so good at organizing. I wonder if she saw anything in my writing abilities too. She probably would have told me, but we didn't really do that much writing in her class that year. Did you do a lot of writing in fifth grade? Anyway, I am so excited I signed up right away and I can't wait to go home and tell my mom. She'll be so proud." I finally breathe.

Leslie was just about to open her mouth when I accidentally speak at the same time, "Well, aren't you going to say something?"

"Yes, of course I'm going to say something. Like, congratulations, and, of course, you're a really good writer. I've seen your handwriting. You know you have the best penmanship of anyone in the seventh grade. You make me laugh all the time. I bet if you can get a column where you write funny stories, you'd become queen of the school. And I could be your royal princess, as we stride down the hallways together, just knowing that all those looks coming our way are because we are popular, and not because people are laughing at our seal barks." Leslie is the best friend in the world. She really knows how to make me feel good.

"Okay. I'll call you when I get home, right after I tell my mom. She is going to be so proud." Excitedly, I run to the bus line where I am one of the last few to board. It doesn't matter where I sit because I daydream the whole way home.

The bus pulls up to Lexington Street, not quite a mile away from where I live. I can run home today because most of my books are in my locker and my book bag is lighter than usual. I have a fetish, my friends say, about book bags. I never can seem to find just the right one to help me feel like all of my materials are perfectly at my fingertips. The big, floppy canvas bags that are built like an over-the-shoulder duffel bag are just too deep for me to find pencils when I need one. They also become so heavy because, with all that space, I can stuff practically all my text books plus my binders for each class into the whole thing. I have to adjust my walk in order to support the weight. It feels as though I am hauling rocks from the prison quarry.

This is the fourth bag I've succumbed to buying this trimester. When the season changed from fall, the brown and golden-hued bags went away, and I was bedazzled by the ruby and other gem-like duffels that came out in time for the holidays. Of course, with everything on sale, I couldn't resist the temptation that both the ruby red and kelly green bags induced in me. I figured it quite reasonable to have both. That way I could always save the green one for spring, or St. Patrick's Day, and spare my scarlet satchel from overusage into the third trimester.

The problem is, I didn't investigate the inside pockets deeply enough because I later discovered that with so many built-in slots for small binders, calculators and two text books, I could never haul my entire locker's contents on the weekends when I wanted to get ahead on my class projects. I was limited. And the thing I hate most about bags is feeling that I cannot work within the space I have been given. Therefore, I end up switching frequently. Even though today I am carrying my favorite blue, the color of pool water sparkling on a clear day, I know it, too, will go by the wayside as soon as summer yellows start rearing their heads.

"Mom, I'm home. You'll never guess what." I barrel through the door. I find her sitting sprawled flat out on her bed, poring over her wrinkles in her hand-held magnifying mirror. This is her daily routine. After "Days of Our Lives" and "The Doctors," and before the "20,000 Dollar Pyramid," she stares at what used to be smooth skin but is now thick and coarse with patches of brown spots bigger than freckles on her cheeks and forehead. It's the same face every day. I don't know what good it does to examine it over and over again. But I decide this is something I ought not to state out loud. Instead, I offer up my good news to take her mind off the mirror.

"Mr. Koker, my science teacher, told me my writing is so good that he wants me to sign up for Journalism because he is going to start a school newspaper and he thinks I could be in charge of one of the departments after I get a little experience. This is such a big deal because the eighth graders are all going to want to be writing for the newspaper just so they can be popular. But they probably aren't even talented enough to be good writers." I breathe.

"Now, didn't Mr. Koker just give you a C minus on your last report card? Why would a teacher who thinks you are only average, and nearly below average, give you a job on the school newspaper? Perhaps you misunderstood him. Was he just trying to be nice to you, do you think?"

She does have a way of gently pointing out the obvious. How could I have overlooked this? Maybe Mr. Koker was just being nice.

He seemed to be telling me a secret that nobody else knew. He sure did go out of his way to make me feel real important. Maybe he's trying to give me confidence so I'll do well on the microscope test on Friday. I feel my forehead crinkling because now I am confused. Maybe I did get it backwards. But I know I'm a really good organizer; everyone knows that. Why would he say that, plus everything else, if he doesn't really mean it?

"He sounded like he meant it. He did say that eventually I could maybe be in charge of one of the departments. I don't know. I like Mr. Koker. I think it would be fun to work on a newspaper. I like to tell stories. Maybe some of the kids would think my stories were funny. Leslie thinks I will do a great job." I immediately wonder if I have somehow said too much, judging by the way her face was beginning to twitch on the left side.

"Has Leslie ever had experience working on a newspaper? Why doesn't she sign up? She gets all As. Her mother must be really proud of her. With her good looks and brains, she will really make something special of herself in life. I think she might actually decide she'll want to be in Journalism, too, once she goes home to tell her parents that you wanted to sign up. You better watch out for her. She may be the one getting the big column. And she will have deserved it, too, because she is attractive and she earns good grades. I really can't see how Mr. Koker thinks a C minus student would be the best person to be writing for the school newspaper. Perhaps you can ask him if there is another elective that would suit you better."

And somehow I realize the conversation is over and it is time for the "$20,000 Pyramid" to begin.

The show's theme music begins in the background as I shuffle down the hallway to my room. I slump on the edge of my bed and wonder how I went from being the happiest ever ten minutes ago to now feeling like I should apologize to Mr. Koker for getting it all so mixed up in my head? Instead of calling Leslie, I decide I will feel better if I take a nap before I start my homework. I lie down and, within seconds, I am fast asleep and never even hear the phone ring when Leslie calls two hours later.

I awaken in time for dinner, to which I am greeted by the warm and familiar banter of my father after a long, hard day. My father is a big sales manager for his company. He is in charge of a lot of states and has to travel a few days at a time throughout the month. It usually works out that on Sunday afternoons, after church, he is packing his briefcase and monogrammed suit bag. The taxi begins tooting its horn around supper time. Then, it's a long week with him away, and I am usually the first one to throw open the door on Thursday nights, when I hear the taxi slamming the trunk after unloading the luggage for its fare.

Today, my dad is home for dinner for the fourth night in a row. This is his off week, and we are planning a night out as a family tomorrow to eat at Sizzler, which is usually only reserved for birthday dinners, but my dad got a raise so we're celebrating. Every day he comes home and he goes through a little cheerleading ritual with us kids. It starts off with him asking, "How's your P.M.A. today?" which means our Positive Mental Attitude, and we're supposed to respond with the company slogan, "I feel happy, I feel healthy, I feel terrific!" At the ending part, if we're really doing it right, we sort of swoosh our elbow across our midsection and give a lucky snap at the end. It shows enthusiasm.

At first glance, my dad checks my P.M.A., and I start to cry. He sort of saw it coming, and gently probes as to what could be the matter. I explain to him that I think I made a mistake about something my teacher said and, when he asks for details, I repeat the story that I relayed to mom after school.

"Mr. Koker is a fine teacher. I remember meeting and talking with him at great length during Back To School Night. He seems very happy to be at Stanyan, and it sounds like he knows a thing or two about talented students. Do you know he taught for five years in Boston before he moved back to California? He taught many students whose parents were professors at some of the best colleges in the country. So when he encourages you to participate in something, I am sure, honey, it's because he sees something special in you that he wants to help you develop. Don't be afraid to try new things, no matter what kind of discouragement or disappointment you might experience along the way." That was the best cheerleading speech I had ever heard.

"I signed up already, dad. I was so excited when Mr. Koker told me that I could be in charge of the eighth graders—eventually, if I became a department leader. I hope I actually get in. There will probably be a lot of people signing up." I throw out this little caution so that just in case I don't actually get picked, we will know it is merely because of available space.

"My pet, I will take your first article to the office to share with the guys. I'll even hang it on my wall. You'll do a great job. I know it." This is enough to get me to zoom through the homework I have ahead and jump into bed with eager anticipation of the next school day.

I find Leslie before our first class and fill her in on the conversations at home. We decide to go to Mr. Koker's room at lunch to see when the names will be posted. He tells us that the list will be on his front door after school and to come back then. But he says it with a grin, so I am feeling confident.

Sure enough, at three o'clock, I find my name near the end of the seventh grade roster, as it appears we are in alphabetical order. There is no calming me down. I am happier than I have been in a long time. This is going to be a life-changing experience. I just know it.

The first assignment Mr. Koker has us write is a free topic that we feel will be worthy of front page news. It needs to be our very best effort because this will help him to determine who will be best suited for which department, and who will be reserved for which page of the newspaper. Usually the least interesting writers appear further back. Best stories are front page, according to Joshua Fields, hunky love monkey.

I wrestle for hours to think of the perfect topic, and finally, it occurs to me, the subject everyone at school will be interested in reading about, students and faculty alike. I make my plan, I do my research and, in a week, I turn in my double-spaced two-page article.

The results are in the following Monday. Mr. Koker wastes no time over the weekend, grading all these submissions between football and shopping with his girlfriend. The announcement comes while the room is so silent you'd think the principal was there, standing over our shoulders.

"Great ideas, guys. I can tell we're going to have a super newspaper, but some of you have original ideas that really merit certain real estate in the paper. Starting with Back Page, Letter to the Editor—Joey Rogers. (Big applause, because we all like Joey's opinions. He led a crusade to kill the menu item of horse hamburgers we were being served last year in the cafeteria, so this is a perfect fit.)

"Third Page, Entertainment, for Nicole Cassidy. (She is the biggest gossip, after all, so this makes perfect sense.)

"Page Two, Stanyan News, goes to Brad Hamilton, (the brainiest brainiac at school. He also discusses current events with Joshua because he subscribes to Time magazine for teens.)

"And the Front Page goes to a journalist who can capture the spirit of what our school is really about. Vandra Zandinski will be featuring a regular column called 'The Greatest Lesson Teachers Learned in School.' We will be running a photo of our teachers from when they were in middle school, and a little bio about who they are now and who was the biggest influence on teaching them a great life lesson during their middle school years. Congratulations to you all!"

Mr. Koker beams, and he gives me a little wink, as if to say job well done. That's all I need for the day. I run with this for the rest of the year and do my school newspaper proud. My department gets to know things about teachers they never would have thought to ask if they weren't in the position to do the research. The more my confidence grows in Journalism, the more my grades improve in other classes. I start looking at science in a whole different way. Mr. Koker sees me as such a leader on the newspaper staff that I get to make copies after school, before release days, along with a couple of the eighth graders, who know how to use the copy machines. This is a real privilege. It is like I can do no wrong. I am a new person, and kids think I am good at my job. So does Mr. Koker, which is why the one afternoon he needs to go to the principal's office, he leaves me in charge of the class.

"Class, while I am in the front office, Vandra will be in charge of telling me who is doing their class work and who is not. I'll be back in a few minutes." It is commanding, and with this blanket power I have a surge of self-importance rush to my head like a helium balloon that all of the sudden has enough air to float away on its own, breaking the string that keeps it grounded.

"You heard him. Let's get to work," I say authoritatively from the front of the room. Gosh, everybody looks so different standing up here from this viewpoint. 'Why are they all staring at me?' I silently wonder. I stand just in the same spot where Mr. Koker always teaches from and watch, like a hawk, as the kids continue to do their work, largely ignoring my powerful presence. Until Billy Contreras, the resident smart mouth, pops off with his usual witty comments.

"Yo, teach. I think I'm done for the day. What do you say you give me an A and let me outta here early?" He tries to charm me.

"No. Do your work," is the only logical reply I can think of.

"What are you gonna do if I say I'm not gonna, huh? You gonna make me? How are you gonna do that, teach? Teacher's pet is more like it, anyway. Why do you think Mr. Koker picked you? It's not like you're getting all As, anyway," he kept taunting.

"You know, you could just go to the office, if you want." It is meant to sound so much harsher, but it comes out as weak as the dandelions that blow in the first wind. They lose all their soft needles that amount to so little we can hardly refer to them as petals. They are pushovers from the start, and here I am, my frail blossoms disappearing in the wind with Billy's first gust.

The kids all laugh at me in a mocking tone, and I know I have it coming. But somehow I think I am deserving of a lot more recognition, and the only way I figure I can earn it back and save face with my peers is to wage a battle that will earn me my stripes. Like any commander, I charge in, not knowing the fate that lay ahead.

To take on the biggest bully in our class, I have to show my resolve to take on someone even more powerful. So I start to show some attitude with Mr. Koker. I don't do anything other seventh graders aren't already doing: a few eye rolls, combined with bored gasps when assignments are announced; asking questions unrelated to the teacher's topic; and boldly showing defiance with brainiac questions like, "Why are we even learning about volcanoes if there hasn't been an eruption in, like, a thousand years?"

I think the final straw breaks for Mr. Koker when I challenge him on a question I do not want to answer. He is looking for class participation points, and finally calls on me. I throw out my regular line of, "That's a dumb question. Who cares, anyway?" I figure it is good for a big laugh from the kids in the back row, and I am right. What I don't count on is the eruption from within Mr. Koker that reminds me how powerful volcanoes really are when they eventually do blow their stacks.

"I am sick and tired of this new attitude of yours, Miss Zandinski. I have helped you a lot over this past year, and all you seem interested in doing now is making a fool of yourself every time you open your mouth in this class. I will not tolerate your rudeness and your disrespect, and I'm pretty sure your father will be surprised to hear about your behavior when I call home this afternoon. I don't know who you think you are, but I am the teacher in this room. I've graduated from seventh grade. You need to sit there, listen, take notes and answer the questions I ask with a respectful attitude."

There is spit flying from his mouth, and I can see veins popping from his necktie. I have never heard Mr. Koker yell like this before, except for one time, for only a quick second, when he let the class know we were being too loud. But he railed on me.

I have been slinking in my chair, unwittingly until now. My chin is level with the desk. My feet are hanging out from under my table top about two stride lengths forward in the aisle. If I could have disappeared into the recesses beneath the floor, I would have preferred it. I am embarrassed. Mr. Koker called me on every single offensive account I was guilty of. Even the kids in the back of the room, with their collective, "Ooooooooooh. You were told," are silenced when Mr. Koker snarls at them to shut their mouths.

"Are we clear?" Nostrils flaring, he stands his ground, feet planted firmly. I have seen it many times before on Wild Kingdom, when lions have just finished off their kill.

Hearing this tongue lashing from the one person I admire most is bad enough, but hearing it while he is spitting profusely and scolding me, deservedly, in front of my peers and enemies alike is unforgettable.

At this point, I have no recourse other than to reply humbly and apologetically, with bowed head, "Yes, sir. It's clear."

In this instance, this very moment, Mr. Koker teaches me something about humility and power, and true leadership. I learn many lessons from him. Among them, it is important to rise to meet your potential. If you are lucky, there will be those nearby willing to help you discover it.

It is important to treat everyone with respect, especially when you are in a position of power over them.

Finally, it is critical to not let your successes go to your head, because when you get too big for your britches, there will always be someone there to tell you so.

Eighth Grade with Mrs. Schreiber

Finally, I am one of the eighth grade girls. I still remember what it is like to get picked on as a sixth grader, so I watch for little ones carefully. I am also the editor in chief of Stanyan News. Mr. Koker appointed me in charge for the first semester. He knows how hard I worked last year, and I have become a really good student for him. Leslie Hinton and I are still friends, and with the popularity I gained last year by befriending this sun bleached beauty from San Diego, Maureen Stafford and Molly Donovan want to hang out with me now, too. This year, Maureen and I have classes together, and we talk about Joshua Fields and wonder if he will ever ask her out.

There are a few teachers who are making indelible impressions upon me. Mr. Harold Spork is my Pre-Algebra teacher. I suppose it is Algebra One that I should have been placed in this year, however, my mastery of communicative, associative, and distributive property calculations leaves me flustered, so I need one more year to try and get it right before high school.

Mr. Spork has a name that leaves him wide open to nicknames of the non-flattering sort. While he does wear plaid shirts with short sleeves and khaki pants, or brown polyester pants, no one will call him Mr. Dork. He is far too militant. We mostly fear him, and loathe him, but never the latter outwardly, or he would sniff you out and embarrass you in front of the whole class.

Joshua Fields is in this class with me. He sits in front, two rows over from Mr. Spork's desk. Josh is usually reading the business section of the newspaper by the time the dismissal bell rings because he is such a whiz at math and he can do numbers in his head. He is amazing.

"Joshua Fields," Mr. Spork will begin, "what is Mary's salary if she earns 125% of Joe's income, Tom earns 80% of Joe's, and the total for all three is $61,000?" This starts the blood rushing in the room because we all wait to see if this will be the day that the teacher is able to stump the hunk. It's formal name is "lightning round." It's a quick back and forth answer session Mr. Spork likes to throw out to his more advanced students at the beginning of each class.

While the rest of us do nothing but sit there, silently shrinking in our seats until we become invisible to Mr. Spork, Joshua rebounds with, "The formula is '$x + 1.25x + .8x = 61,000$.' Therefore, $x =$ Joe at $20,000, $.8x =$ Tom for $16,000, and $1.25x =$ Mary earning $25,000, Mr. Spork." Just like that. Magic math. He can do any kind of tricky calculation in his head, and for the really difficult computations that require a calculator, it takes him only a few seconds longer. While we think every day that this is the question that will surely stump him, he again shows up the teacher with the same kind of sporting bravado that Mr. Spork carries. Our teacher likes winners. He does not like weakness, and he can smell fear.

On another particular day, something else has our attention, and it is not the fun and games of Mr. Spork and his pet. Every teacher has a routine. Students know when a teacher is in a good mood or a bad mood. Today happens to be a day familiar to us by now because it usually starts out with the same ominous pattern. Mr. Spork snaps back from his desk and emerges from his rolling chair in mid flight. We know the inevitable doom of that chair. Its metal frame, spurred by the whirring wheels spinning beneath, will sail out of control behind his desk until it finally collides with the chalkboard. There will be a scratching noise as the steel frame scrapes across the green board. We all wince and uniformly avert our eyes. This begins the aisle walking Mr. Spork likes to do while we are to be quietly focusing on today's math assignment. He walks slowly, purposefully, as if he is a field marshal inspecting the ranks, up and down each aisle, slowly picking over the work that every one is struggling to cover with their arms, so as to not give away its inferiority. At least this is my approach. Cover it all up, and he will definitely get the impression that I am buried in my concentration so deeply I can barely take notice that he is trying to sift through my pencil shavings to find a discernible answer.

Mr. Spork is four rows away when I begin to wonder how far behind I might be from the other students. I know I can understand this stuff when I am in my room, working quietly for the whole afternoon by myself, but in class, under pressure, I just begin to stare at the clock and calculate my fate. "Oh, no. There are only thirty-seven minutes left for me to figure out these six problems. Oh, no. Now there are only thirty-four minutes and I still haven't finished the first one. How many minutes do I need to spend on each problem until time runs out?" These are my mental ramblings until I become so nervous that I get caught up in doing the math for how much real time I have left to dedicate to each problem, and before you know it, I'm saying, "Oh, no. I have only twelve minutes left and Mr. Spork is in the next aisle."

I hear the heavy clomping of the field marshal's black work boots as they land hard upon the ivory tiled floors. He walks as if he is actually trying to navigate his way through mud holes. His hands are clenched into a ball of little fists behind his back, and his head cocks about the room as regularly as a rooster looking for kernels of corn to peck. In Mr. Spork's case, he's just checking for cheaters who might feel they are off the hook after his watchful eye has already passed through their aisle.

It's my turn. I feel the thunder beneath my feet amplify up through my legs into my heart, which is now racing so fast I hope I die before Mr. Spork sees what a mess I have made of my paper. I have gotten very little work done since I started counting the clock tickings thirty seven minutes ago.

There is a deep sound coming from Mr. Spork, who is standing directly above and behind me, to the left. I pretend to be frozen. Perhaps if I don't move he will think I am invisible and no longer be able to see me. There is a gruff grumbling noise coming from his throat that sounds like a very dissatisfied "Hmmmmm." However, it is filled with an almost gargle-like quality, and I know he is not going to move on to the next victim until whatever sounds coming from him now become the words he intends for me to hear.

"How long have we been working on this assignment today, Miss Zandinski?"

'Is this a trick question?' I wonder. I know the answer precisely, to the very second, because I have been timing it myself. I venture a response. "Thirty-seven minutes, Mr. Spork." I am somewhat pleased with my exactness. Some kids would have rounded down to thirty-five minutes.

"And what have we accomplished in thirty-seven minutes; not thirty-five, not forty, but thirty-seven whole minutes?" The blood is beginning to curdle in his neck as his face starts to flush that red color it gets when he is trying to explain how to divide fractions for the six-hundredth time that week; I am always glad for the refresher, anyhow.

"Well, sir, I got stuck on this one word problem and I was trying to use the skills you've taught us to draw out the components when I realized I was making all sorts of mistakes. So I kept starting over, and then my eraser marks were making it hard to read. I realized I needed to pace myself and so I started calculating how many minutes I should allot for each remaining problem, when it occurred to me that, sometimes, I do better on my own in my room, thinking about what you taught us that day." I am not quite finished, but I can see his impenetrable glare fixating on me with a look of disgust. Did I say too much? I was just trying to be honest.

"You have got to be kidding me. You just wasted your entire class period staring at the clock, counting the seconds until they turned into minutes, until you could just pack up and go? I bet you don't understand one thing I've taught you this year, which is why you will be in Pre-Algebra again next year as a freshman.

"You have got to be one of the slowest kids I have ever seen, and the fact that you can sit here and tell me you've been watching that old clock for the better part of a half an hour blows me away. Is there anything you are learning in school? I would love to talk to your other teachers to see if you can tell them how much of the day you spend counting their clocks in class. You think you are just going to pack up and go home now, don't you? Well, you're wrong. You've wasted your time in this class, which essentially means you've wasted my time. So you will be staying after school to finish the class work today, for exactly thirty seven minutes!"

He is spewing all over my paper, and now I have tiny little mud-like puddles forming on what was the beginning of my problem solution work. The smeared pencil lead and the spit are all mushed together, and I am sure I'll have to start all over again this afternoon.

'How could any teacher talk to their student like this?' I wonder. I want to ask this question, but I know there is no way I will ever get a reasonable answer. Besides, I am too busy trying to avoid the stares of the entire class, gawking at this display of hostility with their mouths gaping wide open. I am also trying to keep my head held up high so as to give the impression to Mr. Spork that I am paying him full attention while he hurtles insults at me. I keep blinking because the mustache above his lip only catches half of the spit that is traveling from his mouth. It moves faster than water from a fire hose. And I am blinking to keep the tears from welling up in my eyes so my classmates do not see me cry.

I hate crying in front of people. What's anybody ever going to say when they see someone pitiful beginning to blubber? "Oh, it's gonna be okay." Well, usually it isn't going to be okay, and if the person were in my shoes, they would know I have a pretty good reason to be breaking on the inside and melting on the outside. I am mortified. Why do teachers think this is the best way to reach their students? Why do they go into teaching if they hate kids so much? Why do I have to come back to this class ever again?

The dismissal bell rings and everyone hastily packs up, a chore they were too distracted to think about while watching the human sacrifice. Even if they are a minute late to their next class, they will feel it is worth it. This bloodbath is better than any fight on the school grounds. You can witness, up close, the carnage slowly being dissected and torn apart by the predator. The poor animal just has to sit there and die a quiet death while all the other jungle inhabitants remain frozen in their tracks for fear of calling attention to themselves.

There is nothing I can say. Mr. Spork is still standing here as if awaiting some kind of stupid reply on my part. I can't say a word. I start sobbing all over myself while I work to shove my overstuffed binder into my backpack. I don't even bother with trying to zip it. I just carry the whole thing in front of me, with both arms held outward like a mother carrying a two-year-old whose legs and arms are wrapped around her waist and neck. I bolt. The last words I hear are, "You better not forget to be here this afternoon Miss Zandinski. Thirty-seven whole minutes."

Mr. Spork is an evil little man. But, thankfully, there are others who will make this wrong right and still give me something to look forward to in my day. Ms. Gail Flanigan is my Social Studies teacher. And she is a goddess.

It is eighth period and Ms. Flanigan is a welcome sight after Mr. Spork's gargoyle face. I am trying to forget the way it contorts and twists the more angry he becomes. I pull myself together in the girls' room and, when I get to Ms. Flanigan's class, we exchange looks. Mine tries to say, "Please go easy on me today. I just had a rough class."

Her look seems to be in tune with mine, and she reassures me with a wink and an expression that reads, "It's okay, honey. We've all had rough days."

I relax and, in one fell swoop, I rush into my desk as the late bell rings, simultaneously unload my backpack, place my American Revolution book onto my desk, and arrange myself into the proper audience sitting-listening position.

Ms. Flanigan is perched upon the edge of her desk wearing a knee-length pencil skirt that resembles shades of brown paper, the kind that holds sack lunches. She has the longest legs I have ever seen, and makes me hope for legs like that when I grow up. Her stems are crossed, and her ankles wrap tightly around one another. She looks like a human pretzel. There she sits. An elegant lady with ruffled auburn hair cut in a chin length bob that begins to gray at the roots; she doesn't seem to mind one bit.

Ms. Flanigan is a proudly self-proclaimed "gay divorcee," a term that does not apply for most of the other divorced teachers. She wears it well, and reels off a smooth self-confidence. She mesmerizes us with her velvet voice that sounds just like the throaty whisper people get right before they lose their voice completely.

Ms. Flanigan has an artful way of teaching the most boring lessons. She can peel a story, layer by layer, until one of us actually falls off the edge of our seat anticipating the next part of the battle that ends the war. It seems like the whole hour spent in her class amounts to nothing more than ten measly minutes before she's done with you. This is why I love having her for my last class of the day. I always go home in a great mood because she is the best teacher I could ever have.

Today the story begins, "There was a man named Paul Revere. He was not a very handsome man; some might say he was a bit ugly. Certainly, his wife didn't mind, because she was a bit ugly, too. But this man was special, and people in town knew it. Like any great man, he had his enemies, and everywhere he went, he had to wonder if the flattery he received was true or a ruse so that spies could report back about his activities. You see, this man was a trusted government employee. He had a dangerous job that nobody else wanted. What he lacked in looks, he made up for in courage and smarts. He had been able to outwit his opponents many times before, and his new assignment would be his most difficult." She breathes in all the right places to give us pause for thought.

She continues with the story of Paul Revere's ride into the infamous night where he met his match in the dark woods, and how they dueled until he was able to carry on with a bleeding arm and a wounded horse. His last words were echoed through the port town: "The British are coming! The British are coming!"

It is an amazing adventure that we relive through her special features. We wouldn't have learned about his fat wife and how she packed an extra dinner basket for him on his last ride that night. We wouldn't have known about the enemies who lay in wait to try and kill him before he could save the many towns from invasion. No boring old text book would tell us about his courage and selflessness as he narrowly escaped death. Only Ms. Flanigan could sell a story well enough for us to pass the test.

And while she fills a great part of my day with anxious anticipation, there is one other teacher this year who helps me turn a road. It is not by her warmth, or her pencil skirts. It is merely by her exceedingly high standards and no-nonsense approach to writing that I become a hero once again.

Mrs. Doris Schreiber is my English teacher, and she reminds me of a female commandant. She stands, fully erect, at four feet, eleven inches. She is smaller than most of the children in her class, except for Joshua Fields, whose constant weightlifting has stunted his growth. Her hairstyle is cropped closely, like a man's. It leaves only enough length along the highest point of her forehead to create a firm row of bangs that shout, "I know it's a bad cut, but I defy you to say anything."

Mrs. Schreiber never smiles, and she speaks with a German accent. She wears only woolly tweed suits with skirts that hit mid calf. I've never seen her remove her suit jacket, not even on the hottest days. She is all business, all day.

Getting any kind of passing grade from Mrs. Schreiber requires paying full attention in class, excelling in writing on demand within a limited amount of time, and turning in lengthy written assignments full of sparkling wit, and not rifled with any mechanical or grammatical errors. This is the standard for minimum credit only.

To succeed beyond this measure of mediocrity, one must be able to add to class discussions by participating with scintillating remarks, not just those bonehead comments often said underneath one's breath to amuse the boys in the back row. Taking a leadership role in group work or when presenting class projects will also be essential.

But if one desires to rise to the top, where the cream sits, and receive the praise lavished by Mrs. Schreiber as only she can muster with that type of half-smile usually reserved for the stroke ridden, one can feel assured that bragging rights will ensue and an "A" will be rightfully yours.

This is no small accomplishment, and the work required probably rivals that in any college course. Mrs. Schreiber expects that you will do a research report in addition to all the other essays that will be written for class. Your command of the English language must be on a par with Mrs. Schreiber's, and you must be willing to tutor your peers when time permits in class.

This lady needs to be told a few things. Like, first of all, we're thirteen and we have a life outside of English. Secondly, nobody really wants more than a "B" if we can get an "A" in P.E. to balance out our grade point average to make honor roll. Finally, relax a little. You're making us nervous wrecks. Let's have some fun. We're eighth graders, after all. There's time for hard work next year, when we're in high school. This lady needs to be told a few things, but I'm not going to be the one to do it. I have a really good reputation with my teachers right now, and I'd sort of like to keep it that way.

The first assignment is to write an essay using our creativity. We can be as imaginative as we want. What to write about, I do not know, but that song on the radio, "Disco Duck," sticks in my head, and somehow it leads me to this idea. So I begin. The title is "Mommy, Grow Up."

I wish my mother would grow up. One day I asked her to make my bed. Her reply was, "No, I hate making beds. I never get to do what I want to do, always what you want." Then she started crying. I told my mother that if she didn't make my bed, I would never talk to her again. So she made it, very neatly, too, I might add.

That evening, I asked my mother very nicely to wash the dishes. Her answer was, "Why do I have to do it? I cooked the dinner!" I told my mother that if she didn't wash the dishes, I would send her to her room. She did them with no problem at all. After that came dessert. I passed out Girl Scout cookies. My mother, of course, wanted more. I told her no. She didn't want that answer, so she lay down on the floor and started pounding with her fists and kicking with her feet, right when I was trying to watch an important interview with Ronald McDonald. I couldn't concentrate, so I turned up the volume and she started fussing even louder. I told my mother that if she didn't shut up I wouldn't take her to Parkside Mall with me tomorrow. She shut up immediately.

The next day was Saturday, so I took my mother to Parkside, as I promised. The first thing she wanted to do when we got there was to go into "Casual Corner" to buy a fur coat. After she bought it, she was so happy that she started to run all over. I was so embarrassed. When we reached the part of the mall where "J.J. Newberry" was, she ran in, stuffed her face with junk food, ran out, ran into "Disco Duck," bought a gold dress and started dancing to the good music they play. I went home. She came home on the bus. Till this day, my mother is still at the age of six, but I love her.

That's it. Simple as that. My homework assignment is complete. I don't know what Mrs. Schreiber will think of it. Right now, I think it's kind of clever, but I have math to worry about next so, until she grades these papers, there's no use worrying.

Two days pass and the little general greets us with her non-smile. All I usually see from her is the center mount of her dentures, but today, she shows me a little more. I can actually see far enough back to count her four front teeth. To what do we owe this fantastic display of warmth? I suppose we will soon find out.

"I want to spend today reading some of your essays aloud. You should have a pretty good idea of what is an excellent essay and what is considerably sub par. So, I expect for you to be quiet, I expect for you to be polite, and to keep any negative remarks to yourself because it might be your abysmal essay that I choose to read next time."

She picks three essays. The first is about a little girl who gets lost in a forest and has to find her way back by following a trail of bread crumbs. I know this story sounds familiar to me, but I figure it must be a coincidence. Apparently, it is filled with plagiarism, which means the author, Cindy Sullivan, has to redo the whole thing and the most she can get is a "C." That's rough. But that's Mrs. Schreiber.

The second essay is one that Mrs. Schreiber holds high in her hand waving it proudly and snapping it in place, positioned right beneath her seeing glasses, which are perched so far upon her sniffer that I fear they might actually slip off that bud she calls a nose. When she begins with, "There are many times I remember seeing rainbows, but this one is the prettiest by far …," I know it isn't my essay. Yes, it is lovely, and rather dull. There is no personality, no pizzazz, and if that's the kind of thing Mrs. Schreiber likes, then I am never going to get the "A" I secretly want. The essay went on and on about the beauty of nature on a camping trip with her family. La ti da di da. Is it done yet? The great honor for that one goes to Denise Hamilton. She's Brad Hamilton's younger sister, but she's so smart, she skipped a grade. So now, everybody who doesn't already know asks Brad, if Denise is his twin. He gets so annoyed.

Finally, the third essay. Mrs. Schreiber begins without any introduction. How are we going to know if it is good or bad unless she tells us? Immediately, it starts. "I wish my mother would grow up." Oh, my gosh. It's mine. I try not to pop out of my seat because I do not want to be embarrassed in her class. Mr. Spork is rough and mean, but Mrs. Schreiber is someone I respect, even though she is a little too harsh, and I do not want to make mistakes in her class. Is it good or is it bad? Oh, please don't let this be the day that kids start laughing at me. As if on cue, I hear the giggles begin emerging from several people in different rows of the room. Did they find out it was mine? Are they making fun of me already? Did I miss something funny? And then it becomes clear. Mrs. Schreiber, herself, cannot keep a straight face when she gets to the part about the Mommy walking into Disco Duck to buy gold jewelry, dancing to the popular music. I didn't think it was this funny, but because she is laughing, the whole class feels free to laugh out loud, and I become giddy with relief.

The essay finishes and Mrs. Schreiber asks the class why we laughed? Many of the kids say because the mom acts just like the kid and the kid has to act like the mom. "Yes. That's what we call irony, and when it is written well, it does make us laugh. How do we know if it is good or bad?" she probes. A few hands shoot up in the air.

"If we laugh at the funny parts, it's good. If we laugh because it's stupid, it's bad," the genius in the back states proudly. Again, I wonder if these guys are laughing because they like it or because it's stupid.

Finally, Mrs. Schreiber solves the mystery. "Good writing surprises you because it makes you laugh, or cry, when you least expect it. This is good writing, and I am pleased to say it belongs to Vandra."

The whole class applauds. Wow, I am so happy. I have never been this happy before in school. This even tops the time when the eighth grade class president said he would go to the Sadie Hawkins

Day dance with me. And he was cute, too. This is a great day. 'How can tomorrow top it?' I wonder.

My year is on a great roll so far. I remain editor in chief through first semester and hand it off to someone else when we return from Christmas Break. I know in my heart no one will work as hard as I did helping everyone brainstorm creative ideas to write about. Probably no one will boss them into meeting their deadlines, either. I even typed some of their pieces just to make sure they made it into the winter edition.

Mr. Koker thinks I've turned into a great newspaper woman and he has become one of my best teachers. Leslie and I are still really close, but Maureen and I are becoming best friends, too. I don't know how to have two best friends, so I try very hard to not hurt their feelings when I get invited to Leslie's house if Maureen wants me to do something, too.

A few really big things happen to me before the year ends. First, there is a huge contest in our local newspaper sponsored by the Rotary Club. The prize is $100 and a plaque that the Rotary gives you. You also get to have your piece in the local paper along with your picture. I didn't know anything about this contest, but Mrs. Schreiber did. She pulled me aside one morning before class to tell me that she submitted her favorite poem of mine I had recently written. She thought it was good enough to be considered seriously, but the competition was for middle schoolers and high schoolers, so it might be tough to win. The fact that she thinks enough of my work to enter me is prize enough. She makes me feel so proud, even though my entry is not "seriously considered." I have never had another teacher like her. She pretends to be so mean on the outside, but on the inside she is so kind. Usually, when teachers pretend to be mean on the outside, you find out they're not pretending.

The next big thing to happen to me is Stanyan's own writing contest. It is open to all three grade levels and there will only be one winner chosen for each grade level. No Honorable Mentions, just straight first place winners. The stakes are high because there are a lot of articles being submitted. Mrs. Schreiber's advice is to submit my "Disco Duck" story. Out of 187 entries for eighth grade alone, I win. I cannot believe it. My story runs in our school paper, along with the other two winners. People in all grade levels are quacking to me every time they pass by. I feel like a local celebrity.

And if this isn't notoriety enough, I am asked by Mr. Koker to create an original poem for the school paper that will capture the sentiment of eighth graders as we say goodbye to Stanyan Middle School. I agree right away, without having a clue what to write. And then, of course, I am inspired. The memories I have had this past year with Leslie Hinton spark an idea and I am off and running. I write it in Journalism class and, before I get to the middle, the tears begin to flow. It is called "Friends Will Be Remembered," and it is reserved for the front page of our last issue. As the typewriters stop clicking away, other people come to read over my shoulder and walk away whispering, "That is so good, Vandra." A hero, once again.

The story runs, the issue comes out and people are complimenting me left and right. Even teachers are saying nice things to me. I'm going to miss everyone at this school. And then it hits me.

As I am walking into Mrs. Schreiber's room, I realize I have forgotten to put my last big assignment in my backpack the night before. I have nothing. She absolutely does not accept late work. I try to explain to her, hoping that she will forgive me this one time because she likes me so much. Boy, am I wrong.

"Miss Zandinski, I do not play favorites. You have done a remarkable job in this class, but you will earn your grade just like everyone else and you will get no special allowances from me. Is that clear?" Crystal.

I can not believe that after all my hard work in this class, she is holding one little essay over my head as if I am a lazy nonperforming student. Whose essays does she think she's been reading aloud all year? If it weren't for me, no one in this class would have been half as entertained. How dare she?

Maureen Stafford is reading my mind, and says just about as much in a long note she passes to me from across the aisle. Maureen's note is filled with her rantings about how unfair Mrs. Schreiber is being to me. I agree, and have plenty to say on the subject on my note back to her.

"I have had enough with trying to be a goody two shoes all year long in this class. If she isn't going to give me a chance to turn in that stupid essay, then she is not my favorite teacher anymore. In fact, she is probably one of the meanest people I know. I think I already hate her. And her ugly wool dresses." And I go on and on and on, until I feverishly fill two pieces of binder paper. I am a writer, after all. As I carefully assemble the note by folding it into quadrants, and mini quadrants, and penning Maureen's name on top, marking it "Top Secret" and "Urgent," outlined by little daisies, I wish I had spent as much time on my plan for tossing it across the aisle. Mrs. Schreiber waltzed right over to Maureen and snatched it out of her hands.

Death to me. Oh, how can I be so stupid? Now I'm really going to be in hot water. And what makes it even worse, the part that Maureen wrote to me starting this whole thing is still in my backpack. There wasn't enough room for me to reply on her paper, so I started my own. Now it looks to Mrs. Schreiber as if I began the whole evil note business. Oh, I think I'm going to cry.

Instead of saying anything to either of us, Mrs. Schreiber reads the note silently to herself while the rest of the onlookers curiously gaze upon her, trying to read that wrinkly face for any sign indicating how deep my trouble might be. She finally finishes, both pages, and walks carefully, with her stapler, to the back bulletin board while dragging a chair behind her. She stands high upon that chair and secures my note to the wall at eye level for the tallest kid in class to read. She then staples the second half of the note right next to it. Together, they hang for the remainder of the day, which is the whole day, since I have her second period. I am mortified. I ask her if she realizes that the note is about her, and doesn't she feel embarrassed putting it up when I said such mean things.

"We'll see who becomes embarrassed, Miss Zandinski." She gruffly turns her back and allows the murmuring to die down while we get back to the real work we are supposed to be finishing before the bell rings.

When it is time to pack up, everyone makes a beeline for that note. They laugh, but this time I can hear the difference in the tone. Instead of feeling like I am funny, I can hear kids saying, "Busted!" while they head out the door bursting into laughter, rushing to find their friends. There is no glory in this for me.

At this sinking moment, I learn something invaluable that only

Mrs. Schreiber can teach me. No matter how hard you work, you are only as good as your last job. This note might not ruin my reputation for great writing, but it will definitely cement a new impression upon my beloved teacher. I truly do love her, and I got sucked into an angry moment that was fueled by a friend who egged me on.

I have learned that no matter what other people think, it's important to remember the people who help you to find success and victory. And that you should never say anything about them behind their back that you can't say to their face.

Finally, whenever you put something in writing, there is a chance it may come back to haunt you.

Dear Mrs. Schreiber forgives me before the end of the school year. But I never forgive myself for hurting a little old lady like that, especially after mentoring me the way she did. I should be ashamed. And I am.

Ninth Grade with Mr. Harris

Chapter 11

It is not that big of a dilemma for me to decide that public high school is not the place I want to continue spending the rest of my education. I do not wish to relive the torture inflicted upon me from those horrible eighth grade girls who are now lurking, waiting for my arrival at Bennion. My new best friend, Maureen Stafford, has been planning to attend the private girls' high school that all four of her sisters graduated from, so when she asks me if I'd consider going to Trinity with her, I can't say 'yes' fast enough. The only stumbling blocks I might run into will be getting my folks to agree to pay for private high school, and getting in with my troubled math scores.

It turns out my parents are secretly thrilled that they will be having a daughter graduate from Trinity. And, because of the costs incurred by my new braces, a potential college fund and, perhaps, a wedding some day, they not so secretly decide that I will now be receiving the inheritance I might have otherwise enjoyed in fifty years.

Meeting Sister Paula only reminds me of the nuns from Montessori. Trinity happens to be adjacent to my former preschool which, from my bird's eye view, sits atop a little drive at the back entrance, encased in a grove of fragrant Eucalyptus trees. There, upon a sloped green field for play between us, I can still see my old friend, the yellow swing set.

Sister Paula reminds me nothing of Sister Mary Catherine. In fact, she is broad and warm, and has a smile that says, "We welcome you and hope you will enjoy your stay here for the next four years. You are a sister and a daughter to us now." I sort of like this idea. I have never felt this embraced, even from my own mother and sister. For instance, last year, there was a special on PBS about wolves in the wild. I had just read Jack London's *Call of the Wild* in Mrs. Schreiber's class, and we also went on a field trip to see his ranch in Sonoma. I told my mom to let me know when this special was coming on so I could tune in. It happened on a random Tuesday night. I was in my room doing homework when I heard howling coming from the master bedroom. I wondered what was going on and thought it might be the wolf special so, with great anticipation, I scurried in and found, to my great disappointment, the show ending, credits rolling.

My mom and my sister had been enjoying a bowl of popcorn, exchanging bays at the moon, and learning about the ways of the wolves together. They learned that wolves travel in packs. My mother was now "Timbaku" and my sister's new name was "Kimba." These are wolves that were featured in tonight's episode. I sort of get excited and ask what my new wolf name will be.

"Well, dear, there is not another wolf that survived, so there is no name left for you," is all the matter of factness she needed to make her point. My sister was seated on the floor with the popcorn bowl between her knees just looking up at me without any real registry of emotion. I could tell she wasn't really into the wolf thing, but she sure did like the spotlight that she was sharing with mom. She would probably worm this into a mother-daughter shopping trip after school tomorrow.

I was more sad for the wolf that died than I was for myself. But somehow, I made it all the way to twenty three seconds, while I ambled down the long dark hallway to my bedroom, before the tears started to flush. Darn those wolves when they die. The howling continued, and I shut my door.

Yep, Trinity is sounding like a grand place. A place where I am accepted as a sister and a daughter. I can't wait.

Taking the entrance exam is a big deal. It is filled with all sorts of questions about English and Math and Social Studies and Science. I remember a lot of the things Mr. Koker taught me, and I struggle to punch out Mr. Spork's image every time I come to a word problem. Who really cares what time the train arrives if the car leaves the station at the same time, traveling at a rate of less than half the speed of Amtrak. I do not see why this is relevant.

I am also to write an essay on why I want to attend Trinity and what kind of contributions I think I will make to their good reputation as a student. I am filled with passion while writing this essay. It is long, and with my excellent penmanship, that passes easily for adult forgery, it is a sight to behold. I will get in if this contest is based on my writing skills alone. The next step is an interview with me and my parents, separately and together. This will probably be the thing that kills my chances.

My mom can be so outspoken. She embarrasses me so much. She'll talk to anybody, complete strangers, about anything. It usually revolves around me and how I wet my pants at a neighbor's house once when I was four because I was too polite to not interrupt her conversation with the lady of the house. I love these kinds of stories, especially when told in my presence. They paint me in such a favorable light.

In fact, I wish she wouldn't save just the pee-pee stories for complete strangers, she should unload all our family secrets and expose the insanity that lives within our house on a daily basis. Let everyone in on the good laugh we have every morning when mom starts banging pots and pans in the kitchen at six a.m. as her way of sending dad on his merry little way to work. That's better than any cheery, "Have a good day, dear," wouldn't you think? My sister says our problems are not as bad as the Southland's who are among the prominent families on the block. Their dad dresses in women's clothes, and the mom knows. Wow! I had no idea.

We meet in the parlor, attached to the Principal's office. I feel like we should be sitting down to tea. There may as well be a butler and a silver coffee service. I definitely want to get in to this school.

I think it will be much better for my education rather than going to a high school where the teachers are hanging out on the back driveway smoking pot with the seniors.

The school sends me on my way with one last word of foreboding. "Now, dear, you will be receiving your results, along with our decision about your application, within a few weeks. We wish you the best of luck." Everything that Sister Paula says sounds so formal.

It feels like longer than three weeks. I have been marking off the calendar when twenty-one days arrive and still no mail from Trinity. What has been holding the attention of my other family members, and particularly my father, is the crying jag my mother has been on for the past two weeks. She refuses to speak to anyone in the family and is taking dinners in her room. I don't know what set her off this time, but this is the longest I have ever seen her go without giving in to somebody. I really think if one of us was bleeding to death or gasping for air after having accidentally fallen into the pool she would still stay shut up in her bedroom without a jot of interest in the nearly departed.

I don't get it. Maybe all mothers are like this. Maybe I'm actually lucky. I could have a mother down the street who is standing by as her children watch their father practice his Miss America routine in a ball gown. I should count my blessings.

Between a lot of slammed doors and angry glances and "Harrumphs" being snorted from my mother, I arrive one day to find my dad already home early from work and waiting for me. He tells me before I barely make it through the front door that he and I are going out for an early supper, just the two of us, to his favorite Chinese restaurant, which soon becomes our favorite Chinese restaurant.

I feel so special and so excited. It is a rare treat that he is home any more than a half-hour before supper with the family, and I love spending time with my dad. He always tells me a story with a funny part at the end. The story can be short and very memorable, but I enjoy the longer ones more because all the suspense gets stretched out and the characters really come to life. I have a hard time sitting still because I am anxious with anticipation to see if my predictions actually come true. There seems to always be a twist I don't see coming just when I think I've figured it out. So really, while these are funny stories, there are mysteries involved as well. Maybe this is why my dad likes the Pink Panther and Inspector Clouseau so much.

With this news that we are going out, I want to change into a different after-school outfit. It's a girl thing. I tiptoe gingerly by the door that barricades my mother behind it. I really do not want her coming out to ruin the whole gleeful mood because my dad and I are stealing away for an early bird supper, alone.

In the station wagon, he does the usual P.M.A. check and I tell him I am getting very excited to graduate from eighth grade and that I really hope I get into Trinity. Maureen and I are making all sorts of plans to sign up for all the same classes, and since her sisters have already become familiar with the teachers, it will be so much easier for me to know how to fit in. I am practically squealing with delight. I just know I am getting in.

We arrive at the restaurant in just the short fifteen minute jaunt it takes to wind down the twisting road that leads from my quiet neighborhood in the hills to the cafes and book shops downtown. Once inside, we are greeted and seated without a moment's delay. I am so thrilled to be here with the only other happy member of my family that it doesn't occur to me there might be some kind of reason for tonight's little outing.

"Vanny, the mail came." Yikes. I had no idea. No one has said a word about mail. I sort of expected that the letter would arrive, somebody would probably open it, even though it might be addressed to me, and it would be on my bed when I arrived home from school. Not a lot of drama. I hold my breath while blurring the words together, "From Trinity? What did it say? Did I get in?" I need to breathe, but I am not sure what is happening. Is this good news or bad news?

"Well, let's find out together. I have the envelope right here. I thought it might be nice for us to have a little father-daughter meal together while we determine what the next four years will be like, wherever you may be going." He says it with such a warm smile, as if to say, "Be encouraged, hope for the best, but don't consider it the worst scenario in the world if you have to switch your plans."

He pulls the envelope from the inside coat pocket of his work blazer. I like the way my dad dresses. He is older than most dads, so his style is a little more old-fashioned. Between the look of his her-ringbone camel blazer and soft blue button-down shirt against his darkly complexioned olive skin, and how he smells when he com-bines gargling with Listerine and Wrigley's Spearmint Chewing Gum, I would say he is dashing.

The envelope he pulls from the small, inner pocket of his blaz-er is folded into thirds. I am not sure how he is able to keep it con-tained in that tiny space, typically reserved for a small notepad and the few remaining sticks in a pack of gum. Perhaps that pocket is like a secret drawer and it can hold more than it appears. As he unravels this manila envelope, I can see the postmark was received yesterday, and clearly, it is addressed to my parents, not to me.

All of this is happening in slow motion, as I wait for fate to take its course. He runs the long plastic chopstick from the place setting along the side where the flap has been sealed. There is a wide length of clear tape across the seam to be sure it is extra secure. I feel like I am watching when Charlie and Grandpa are ripping the jacket off of the last Wonka bar they can afford. Will Charlie find the only remaining golden ticket to get into the Chocolate Factory?

"Dear Mr. and Mrs. Zandinski," the letter begins as he reads, and I follow along, "It is with tremendous pleasure that we extend this invitation to your daughter to become a graduating member of Trinity High School, Class of 1983.

"We want to further congratulate Vandra on her marvelous achievement of excelling in the written portion of her entrance examination, and, accordingly, we will be placing her in Honors English, a recommendation not usually reserved for freshmen. Her other classes will be scheduled at a later date.

"Enclosed, you will find the pertinent documents that will require signatures, and health information for Vandra, which will remain on file in our Student Records office. We ask that all of these admission papers be returned to our Registrar before July 16, so that we might be able to process Vandra in a most expedient and efficient manner.

"The Sisters of Trinity are enthusiastic about having such a bright young addition to our school. I am sure Vandra will go far in her education and look back on this experience as a positive spring-board to her future life as a contributing member of our society.

"We welcome you and Vandra, as we will be seeing much of you in the coming years. Please plan on joining us for Freshman Orientation on the West Lawn on August 10 at 5:00 p.m. for our barbeque, sponsored by the incoming seniors. Until then, congratulations!

"With Warmest Regards,

"Sister Paula Butier."

"Dad! I'm in! I'm really in! Can you believe it?" I am trying to maintain my indoor manners and not spill my water or tumble out of my chair, but I can hardly believe it. "I'm in! And I got Honors English! Wow! Mrs. Schreiber will be so proud of me. Dad, did you think I was going to get in?" I ask the question, but I'm not really sure I want to know the answer.

"Honey, I always believed that you had a pretty good shot. Your persuasive letter was very sincere and very convincing. I know you said the math portion was harder than you had hoped, but sometimes a school can overlook a few weaknesses if there appears to be real potential there for you to achieve something. I had a pretty good hunch you'd get in, but when the envelope arrived yesterday, your mother and I knew right away." He has that twinkle in his eye that just makes the whole room around him illuminate.

"How did you know? I couldn't tell anything special about a plain yellow envelope." Now he had my curiosity aroused.

"It's an old salesman's trick. If you are interested in signing a contract with somebody, usually you send them an envelope with a contract, or a lot of papers that require their signature, so the person knows you want to do business with them. If there is no interest, there is no need to include all the paperwork, so a smaller, regular sized business envelope with only a single sheet of paper will do. It doesn't take much paper to write, "Sorry, there is no interest at this time. Please contact us again in six months.""

My dad is so smart. I never would have known this. Imagine all the little things I learn from him. Who else would have taught me this?

The conversation turns to talk of Trinity and dates we need to put on the calendar, and finally we come to finances. My dad pulls out his calculator so he can show me how much the annual tuition is a year and what that really means to the family budget every month.

"Honey, your mother and I will make the adjustments necessary to afford this terrific opportunity, but you have to realize what a valuable experience this will be and you need to apply yourself and work your very hardest. I want to know that you are invested in this even when it gets to be tough, because it will get harder as the years roll on. This is my obligation to educate you so you can become better prepared for adulthood, but it will be your responsibility to make school a priority and keep us posted on how you are doing. We absolutely want to see you succeed. Your mother and I both are so very proud of you."

He glows when he speaks to me. I see his eyes moisten many times when he is giving me "father's counsel," as he calls it. I am inspired to do my very best. I will work hard every night, and weekends too. I will take great notes. I will find study partners. I will ask Maureen's older sisters for help, too. I know there will be difficult tests, and hard teachers, but I know I can make this work. I am saying as much out loud, when I have to ask something else.

"Why isn't mom talking to anybody? I don't think she really loves me. She is always making me feel like I am not very important." My voice sort of cracks at the end and now I am sorry I ask because I don't think I want to know the answer.

"Of course your mother loves you. She's your mother and she wanted to adopt you kids very much. And so did I. She's got her problems because she didn't have a very happy childhood. Have compassion for her and realize she's doing the best she can. She was so relieved to know that you got in because she knows how much it means to you. In fact, she suggested that I take you out for supper tonight so we could open the envelope together. She's at home making dinner now for the rest of the kids."

He is so heartfelt in his sentiments, it makes me want to go home and give her a hug and tell her I love her, too. I don't ask a lot of other questions. Right now, I want to enjoy dinner with my dad and the happiness of us being together. I am listening to his next story, and this is a real good one in the series of the Menahoonies, a village people who live in the Hawaiian islands, and their escapades trying to lambaste the giant known as Prince Punhi-Punhi, who lives nearby.

When we arrive home from dinner, I meet my mom in the kitchen, and I revel in glee to her, "Mom, are you happy I got into Trinity?"

"Well, it got me talking again, didn't it?" Perhaps not the round of enthusiasm I was looking for, but it's an answer that says I am worth her coming out of her room and rejoicing in this occasion. She gives me a hug. She does give great big hugs. She wraps her thick arms around me and pulls me close into her bosom. She holds me for a minute longer than I need to detect that her hair is due for a shampoo and the skin from her cheek is dewy, as though she has just freshly moisturized.

I go to bed knowing that tomorrow everything will be sunnier, even if it rains.

Fast forward to the days approaching the start of freshman year at Trinity. Maureen and I decide to go check out the campus a little ahead of everyone else, and also buy our uniforms, and possibly get a deal on some of the used books incoming sophomores are now trying to unload. As we drive along the tree-lined street that is freshly paved, we behold the campus. It reminds me of the Ivy League schools I have seen on posters in Maureen's sisters' rooms. Her family is really big on education. Her dad is a professor at Stanford University, so all the children are expected to go to big schools, and even get Master's degrees before they get married. Her parents are really strict. No friends are even allowed to call between the hours of six and seven o'clock, because this is when the family has their dinner. Once, Sandy called over there, forgetting to check the time, and she was gently reprimanded for calling during their evening meal. I am so glad it wasn't me. I remember how confused I was when the first time I called Maureen about a homework question, a lady said, "Good Evening, Stafford's." I thought I misdialed a restaurant. Then, I realized her mom is sort of fancy and answers the phone the old-fashioned way, like they used to do in the movies.

As we pull through the iron gates that connect to ivory pillars, we know we are at the right place. This feels like a beautiful fortress, and all we see are goddesses walking around trying to sell us used books. There is the most perfect looking girl with blond hair the color of coral. She has big apple cheeks and wide blue eyes that off-set a dazzling white smile. She is the poster girl I believe Trinity has sent to reaffirm that if we want to look like her, we will study hard and work on our internal goddess potential. Her name is Suzy Penman. She is the perfect Suzy. She is bubbly, tiny and very good at making us feel welcome. We find out later that Suzy is the head cheerleader for her class. I don't understand yet why an all-girls high school has cheerleaders, but I'm sure it has something to do with finding our inner goddess.

I want to be just like Suzy, so I buy all of Suzy's used books and I find out where Suzy got her saddle shoes, so I can get some too. She is clearly flattered by all the attention she gets from awkward freshmen, and I am in line with the many. Suzy asks me who my teachers will be, and I can't remember any of their names. She tells me that I will quickly figure out who I will need to be on my guard with and who are the popular, fun teachers.

I can't wait for the first day of school. I hope I see Suzy in the halls, and maybe we can even eat lunch together, with Maureen, of course.

There is no need for me to have set my alarm on the first day of school because my mom is up at oh-dark-hundred banging pots and pans together and screaming at my poor father. Why can't we be like normal people and start off our mornings with warm eggs, strawberry jam on toast and a friendly newspaper? At least allow the radiance of the sun peeking through our blinds or the blaring of our alarm clocks to be the reason we have arisen from such peaceful slumber. I lie in my bed and wonder how many more minutes her tirade will continue. I know my dad has to be leaving for the office soon in order to beat the traffic to the city. I wait four more minutes and, still, she has one more pot to unload against that wall. Can't anybody else hear this, I wonder? Why is everyone else still in bed? Or are they "fake-sleeping" too?

"Honey, I love you. I have to get to the office. I hope you have a good day," he says to my mother as I can hear his keys jingling in his hand while he makes his usual approach to kiss her goodbye on the cheek. I have witnessed what is coming next many times, and I visualize it as I hear those familiar sounds replay all over again.

"Get away from me. You don't love anything but that job of yours." Which is followed by the sound of a pot lid clanging against another pot lid for special effects, emphasizing what will happen to my dad if he does try to give that marital gesture of affection again. Splat! He will be between those two lids as they clang upon his head. Honestly, I don't know why he tries so hard. If I were him, I'd make a beeline for that door twenty minutes earlier every day just to avoid her pre-dawn outbursts.

As I wait for Maureen and her older sister Colleen to pick me up outside my house, I decide that my curb is a little too close to the action on the other side of that front door. So when they arrive, I suggest that, out of courtesy, I will walk to their house so we can all leave together from there. "It will be one less stop for you to worry about," I offer. And I can make a clean getaway without worrying about someone coming outside, screaming on the front lawn in her nightgown.

I put on a cheery face and I anticipate meeting my new teachers and making a slew of friends today. When my dad comes home tonight to check my P.M.A., I will be able to say with true vim and vigor, "I feel happy, I feel healthy, I feel terrific!"

I discover that freshmen are separated from all the upper class-men. We do not share any common instruction, or lunches. So see-ing Suzy again is left to chance after school, when I can catch a glimpse of her in the parking lot, hurdling herself into one of the junior's convertibles while they are whisked away, radio blaring, with nary a glance backwards.

I have a nun who teaches Spanish. She already smacked a ruler down upon the desk of the girl who was still talking to her friend while Sister Ann was trying to instruct. She knows that it is not proper to actually strike the hand of a child with the flat edge of the ruler, but scare tactics involving that ruler cracking upon furniture are not forbidden.

I have a P.E. teacher who looks like a man, but her name is Miss Matthew-Terry. There is nothing I can see to indicate that her name is not, in actuality, just Matthew Terry, without the hyphen. She is teaching us football. Why? Girls don't play football. At least, I have never seen a girls' football team on television. She says we will also be learning gymnastics and water ballet. Now these two sports strike me as something I would, indeed, be made to learn at an all-girls school. But football? I don't get it.

My Honors English teacher is named Mrs. Brady, but she is nothing like the ever popular mom on the series "The Brady Bunch." She is hard core, and even the really smart girls look worried about meeting her expectations in order to achieve an "A." So far, I wonder how I will survive this year.

My math teacher wears a plastic pocket protector for his pen and pencil set in his short-sleeved collared work shirt. He reminds me a lot of my fifth grade math teacher, Mr. Mott, but I am so relieved to find that he resembles nothing of Mr. Spork, whose image still torments me to this day.

I have a Religion teacher and a Science teacher, both of whom are not very interesting, and both of whom scare me far less than my fourth hour teacher.

Mr. Harris wears a rather unkempt shaggy black beard. His plaid shirts, khaki trousers and comfortable brown lace-up shoes set the tone that he is a casual, fun teacher. He must be one of the popular ones Suzy was indirectly telling me about. We are in a large classroom setting for Social Studies, which seats about forty-five desk-chair combinations. I am cleverly placed along the side wall, toward the near back, but not the very last two rows; I do not want to appear so conspicuously invisible that the teacher calls on me the first day.

I blend into the white wall as best I can, with my crisp white uniform blouse and my white lace bobby socks, to go with my new brown and taupe saddle shoes that I found at the store where Suzy said she shopped. I feel relaxed and I am almost on cruise control, knowing that I can wing it with popular teachers as well as anybody else can.

The door slams behind him as he rushes to the center of the room. He doesn't say a word for what seems like five minutes. He is looking up and down the aisles, I think to silence us with his beady black eyes. But he starts picking out girls who are not wearing collared white shirts, a very important stipulation to our dress code, and calling them up front to get their name and the reason why they are out of uniform. Right then and there, he gives them a detention slip and sends them to the office to call home for a proper uniform. The girls, one by one, slink up to the front, first without bringing their books, until he tells them to get back to their desk, bring up their entire earthly possessions, purse, backpack and books included. The remaining girls who are picked off know immediately they will not be rejoining class today and cart their belongings with them sheepishly to the front of the room to collect their detention.

I am so embarrassed for them. A few of them start to cry. How can anyone be so cruel as to write detentions on the first day of school for having a collarless blouse? What kind of a maniac is this man?

"I am Mr. Harris," he begins with a booming voice that, on certain pitches, will rattle the frame of the glass door. "I will be your social studies teacher this year, as we uncover civilizations afar and study the current news events that are shaping our world today. You are expected to come to class prepared each day with your homework completed, your materials at hand and a thoughtful question that might lead us to a provocative group discussion."

He begins rolling up his lumberjack sleeves to reveal furry arms of the same dense black that match his long, wavy, full head of hair. "This man is a furry little monkey," I think to myself, which I should not have done, because I immediately smile, and he notices an improper reaction from his stance way at the front of the room.

"Something funny back there?" All heads in front of me snap back in unison to see who is on the receiving end of this merciless sneer.

"Oh, no. He isn't talking to me, is he?" I think inside my head. "Please, please, please don't single me out today. I do not want to come up to the front of the room. I am trying to make a good first impression. I do not want a detention. Not today."

"What is your name?" he speaks with such authority. I feel like the time I got caught by the manager when I was smuggling my new baby kitten into the grocery store, stowed away in my new crochet purse.

"My name is," quickly cut off by his demand that I stand and begin again. I repeat, "My name is Vandra. My friends call me Vanny."

"Vandra, what is your last name?"

Please, just let me sit down, I beg with my eyes. "Zandinski." I start to motion as if I am ready to sit again. I sweep my hand across the back of my skirt, smoothing it flat against me, instead of crumpled and unearthed from my caboose if I do not.

"I have not said you may be seated. Tell us why you were laughing, Vandra." His glimmer of enjoyment at my discomfort is easily read by the rest of the class as they anxiously await my reply, because they know the more he stays engaged with me, the less time he has to single any of them out for something equally ridiculous.

"I'm sorry, Mr. Harris. I was not laughing at anything in particular. I am just happy to be here, and it sounds exciting the way you just described our curriculum for the year. I like to read about current events, and I have been hoping to learn more." What am I saying? It is just rambling out of my mouth and I do not know if I am even making any sense. I want to crawl under my desk. I suddenly worry that my underpants might be sticking out from beneath my skirt. Sometimes the pleats get folded a funny way, and instead of pointing down, they flip up at the hem. I jerk my hand back to my behind and check to make sure no one can see my flowered Carter's. Thank goodness I am saved from this one humiliation.

"Since you are such a fan of current events, why don't you plan to deliver our first article tomorrow? I expect an article of any political, cultural, economic or scientific event currently in today's forefront to be attached and summarized in 200 to 300 thoughtful words. You will be presenting your article to the class tomorrow, so be prepared to state your opinion as to why this is having an impact on our world now, and why the class should be informed."

His glare is penetrating. He is unrelenting. I am sure he is still speaking, but I only see his lips move. I have lost my hearing. I am feeling faint. I think I have locked my knees into position and I am not breathing. I am very warm. I feel as though I am a chick sitting under the hot lights of the incubator with every one staring at me, wondering when I will hatch out of my shell. I want to say, "Thank

you, sir," but it only reminds me of that catch phrase from fraterni-
ties, "Thank you, sir. May I have another?" that you are supposed to
utter when being paddled by a board. To appear least insolent, I only
reply, "Would you like that double or single-spaced?"

I finally collapse into my chair. I cannot stand anymore. The last
words I hear are, "Class, you all have the same homework as Vandra,
however, I am sure none of us is looking forward to Vandra's presen-
tation more than I."

With that, the bell rings, I sneak out the back door so I do not
have to cross Mr. Harris at the front, and I run to the girls' bathroom. I need to see if my sweat has made my mascara run, and I
need to drink some cold water. I feel sick. How will I ever make it
to the second day? There is too much pressure in high school. Why
did I have to go to a super hard school for high achievers anyway? I
am never going to get into college. I don't even like to read the newspaper. I wish Joshua Fields were here now. He'd know just the article to cut out for me, and I bet if I asked real nice, he might even
summarize it for me, too.

There come more scenes like this from Mr. Harris. He enjoys
the sport of taking girls off guard by putting them on the spot to
defend their position. To create a position. He smells fear. He hates
weakness. He can't stand crying, and he yells if you look to a neighbor to help you with formulating an opinion. Mr. Harris makes my
pulse rush, and some girls throw up before his class. He enjoys making us nervous. He insults us all the time by telling us that the boys
he taught at the last all-male school he worked at were a lot smarter
than us, and we can't get by on our pretty faces if there are no brains
behind our smiles.

Mr. Harris doesn't know that my days start off with loud bang-
ings in the kitchen and that I go to bed every night feeling like a failure because school is much harder for me than it seems to come for
everyone else at Trinity. Mr. Harris wouldn't even care that I have a
mother who likes to throw tantrums. He throws tantrums. He slams
books when he senses no one is prepared with the reading for today.
He slams doors extra hard when he thinks we don't know he is in the
room. He calls on people who don't even raise their hand just to
humiliate them in front of the group. Mr. Harris is a jerk. He treats

us as though we are meaningless and mindless. Doesn't he realize he has his job because our parents pay tuition so he can have a pay-check?

The lesson Mr. Harris teaches me this year is that no matter how good of a job you think you are doing, when it comes to the problem at hand, there are a lot of criticisms you might be subjected to that aren't even related to the problem at hand, if somebody wants to make an example of you.

It won't matter if you are quiet and paying attention; if your collar fell off your blouse, you are out of class for the day and mortified in the process because you will be made an example.

If you are minding your own business reading the assignment and you are called upon to explain what you have just read and why it is important, but haven't yet developed that much of an opinion, you are going to be held to the fire until you can find a position that is worthy of the class's time to acknowledge, and then challenged until you have enough passion to defend it.

I think Mr. Harris is the meanest teacher at Trinity. The only benefit I now have of moving into my sophomore year is that I won't have to have him again.

Tenth Grade with Mr. Harris—Again

Chapter 12

The only bright spot of walking through the cathedral doors of Trinity's grand hallway entrance on the first day of autumn classes is knowing that I have a fresh new start to make this year and an opportunity to create new first impressions with every single one of my teachers. Maureen and I are anxious to see how many classes we have together this year. I am particularly curious to see who the new Social Studies teacher will be. Anything will be an improvement over the tyranny I experienced last year with Mr. Harris.

The class lists are posted, and Maureen and I have the same Advisory Homeroom as Aileen, Diane, Hilary, Zoe and Kate, a few of the popular girls I became friends with last year and introduced to Maureen. We all hang out together now and it is so much fun. These girls have tons of naughty stories to tell us about the times they tried to play tricks on the nuns when they were in middle school and elementary. Usually we are so engrossed in some kind of gossip or the planning of the upcoming dance that the Advisory period quickly passes by without us so much as hearing any of the announcements over the loudspeaker. It's not that we are chatty, it's that we are daydreamers, and we also like to pass notes. Mrs. Schreiber cured me of passing mean and nasty notes about the teacher, but I am still socializing via correspondence.

Somehow, I missed it. I am holding my new schedule with all seemingly perfect teachers, and yet as I walk into my third hour Social Studies class, my heart drops into the pit of my stomach when I hear that familiar voice seething at the girls as they are shuttling rapidly into their seats. How could it be that I have Mr. Harris again for Civics Literature? He taught me World History last year. There is no way I should be in his class again. My expression reads as much, and Diane leans over to tell me that Mr. Hobson, the new Social Studies teacher, got moved to the music department because they lost one of the nuns this summer to a long battle with cancer. 'Oh, how sad,' I think. Sure, about the nun, too. But what about me? This is terrible.

Mr. Harris clears his throat and begins the year with a speech I am sure to never hear again in my life from any other teacher.

"Many of you had me last year for your first time. I know the kind of students you are, and I feel I know the kind of people you are. Sometimes you only see the teacher that we are, and you do not come to know us as people. Let me tell you about this past summer." He speaks methodically, each word hanging on to the last. This is not the rhythm of a light Disney plot sequence, I think.

"My wife and I like to visit a National Park every summer. We have been married for six years, and every one of those summer trips has been her choosing. I figured it was time for me to get a chance to pick a park and, this summer, she finally let me have my way, provided it was a trip we could make in our car, and one that would allow us to visit her parents in Missouri. My wife; she has a sly way of navigating my decisions to suit her desires. This pretty much left us with only two choices, the Lewis and Clark Museum in St. Louis, or the Presidents Monument at Mount Rushmore, in South Dakota.

"We went to explore St. Louis for our honeymoon, since it was the closest and cheapest getaway we could actually get away to after we were married in her parents backyard. We lived with them for about three months while we finished graduate school. When she got her research assistant position at Stanford, which is where she currently works in the Biology Department, we moved. I don't like to disappoint my wife, so South Dakota became the vacation spot we looked forward to visiting after we spent two weeks with her folks in Missouri.

"The long drive out to St. Louis took us about thirty hours, which I broke into four days. Our car is an old half-breed station wagon hatchback with a Beetle engine. It's pretty reliable, despite the fact that the windshield wipers flap instead of swipe, and the muffler has a pretty bad rumble to it. But we get around and, with regular oil changes, I figured it would last us another five years.

"When you're married, you can either find a lot of things to talk about on a long road trip or nothing much to say at all while you listen for the first radio signal to come in through all the static you are mostly getting between Salt Lake City and Kansas City. My wife and I can't find enough drive time to fill the conversations we stir in one another. Sometimes, when it's her turn to drive, she has to pull over because I get her laughing so bad her head starts bobbing and her eyes automatically shut until she laughs herself into a frenzy.

"No matter how dumb I think my stories or jokes are, there is something so amusing in them to her that she acts like she has never heard anything funnier in her life. This only spurs me on, and at times, we sit on the side of the interstate sipping Diet Coke and laughing until there's pop running out of our noses. Sometimes big semis come by and honk to see if everything is okay. We just wave them on and continue to enjoy this break from the world. It is just the two of us, sharing the company we enjoy more than the year before, or the year before that.

"My wife's name is Melissa. She is twenty-eight years old. The day we pulled over to the side of the interstate to have ourselves a good laugh is the day that everything about our vacation, our summer plans, our lives changed. Melissa and I decided we would drive the last four hours until we arrived at her parents' before midnight. We changed drivers because she had been behind the wheel for six hours already. I had driven the early shift that morning for four hours. This is how we made such good time across the country. We tried to drive as much as we could and save hotel money for every other day.

"This night, as I tuned into the talk radio station so Melissa could close her eyes and be soothed by the sounds of political debaters, I also found myself becoming drowsy and decided to turn off the heater so the crisp night air would keep me alert. I don't remember anything that happened next, but there are plenty of people who arrived on the scene to tell me later in the hospital room that I was lucky to be alive.

"I fell asleep at the wheel and swerved into oncoming traffic across the freeway grassland divider. I was plowed over by a semi truck and pinned behind the steering wheel of my car. Melissa was ejected from her seat and thrown two hundred yards. Her skull was crushed and three of her vertebrae were severed. I was rescued with the jaws of life. I have heard the story now from so many rescue workers and hospital attendants that sometimes I feel I can remember this, but I was unconscious at the time, and pronounced dead on the scene.

"Just as the emergency workers were putting me onto a gurney, they checked one last time and felt a faint pulse. This is what saved my life. They figured I had a twenty-five percent chance of survival and they were going to try to fix me.

"My wife was breathing, but her body was crushed. Her legs were both broken and she was very badly cut. Our car had rolled over her after she had been ejected," he continued without missing a beat.

No one spoke. None of us looked at one another, but we all knew that we wore the same expression: jaws dropped, eyes misting over, lips quivering. The fact that this ogre of a man is sharing his death-defying experience with us is so human. How could we not have imagined that he had a life to look forward to outside of Trinity?

"My wife and I were in the intensive care unit for six weeks. The doctors were mostly worried that I would not recover from the extensive surgery they needed to do to rip open my chest and rebuild my rib cage. I have pins all throughout my chest and I will never be able to run again. But I live.

"Melissa spent ten weeks in intensive care and we didn't think she was going to make it. Her brain did not suffer the kind of damage that would alter her personality, or prevent her from still having all the knowledge she has acquired, but her skull was crushed and she needed four surgeries to rebuild her frame. She will never walk again, even after months ahead of therapy and new technology. The doctors say she is lucky to be alive at all and functioning on her own, as far as having the ability to speak and to write and to think.

"I remember her laughter that day. I don't remember much of anything else. I am not over feeling guilty about not just getting to a motel that night. Somehow, all the people who tell me it's not my fault aren't enough to quiet the voice inside my head that says it is. I tell you this story because I am grateful that I still have a life with my wife. I know that sometimes I was too hard on you. I am grateful for a chance to live my life over again. Sometimes we don't get second chances in life, but when we do, we need to embrace the gift. I am looking forward to being your teacher this year. And more than that, I am looking forward to us getting to know one another, really know one another. I want you to be a success. I am here to help you. I feel from the way you look right now, that you might be here to support me too. Thank you for allowing me to share this story with you. Class dismissed."

I have never seen a grown man cry before, except for the time when my dad had to take our sick cat to the vet to have it put down. That was sad. But I have never seen a stranger cry. We don't know what to do. We are trying to keep from blubbering all over the place so as to not make spectacles of ourselves. There are quiet, steady and slow unzippings of tiny purses, from which packets of Kleenex are being pulled out and gently passed around the room. Mr. Harris has us in awe. He is a living medical miracle and he came back to teach. I don't know how I would be able to come back to my life if I felt like I nearly killed my wife, or at least was responsible for her being in a wheelchair.

Mr. Harris teaches me this year that being human means you've got to let other people in. There is redemption for everyone, and no matter how badly you've mistreated someone, you can always turn a situation around if you have a sincere and open heart.

I learn from this beautiful man that even the people who are the meanest on the outside are capable of having great sensitivity. We all hurt. We all bleed. No matter how badly someone has hurt you, you have to find it in your heart to forgive them when they come to you in their most vulnerable moment. I learn Mr. Harris is human. I can't believe it. I have so much respect for him to share such a personal story. He had to stop many times to bite his bottom lip. All I could see were black whiskers from his beard hiding his face, which was cracking under the stares of twenty sophomores. We wanted to rush to his side and hug him, and tell him we were so glad he was here to be our teacher, and everything will be all right. Mr. Harris is a hero in my eyes. He has lost almost everything and yet he is willing to take this experience and become better instead of bitter.

This year, in Social Studies, I may end up reading CliffsNotes for half of the literature assignments we have, but I learn more from Mr. Harris than I can expect to learn from any teacher again. Life is precious. Treat people as if there might be no tomorrow.

Eleventh Grade with Miss Elliott

Chapter 13

Through my high school career thus far, I find that it is not until we are closing the books for the year and getting ready to break for summer that I am finally grasping my concepts. I regularly excel at my subjects, but usually only in the last two months of the academic year. I am like that old glue horse still running races. I always pull through a nose short at the finish. The agony repeats itself as I try to catch my rhythm again with all new teachers and difficult material to master the next year. I am performing well in English classes, but only because I enjoy the essays. When it comes to reading British literature and American authors, I am terribly bored and often too tired from working at Chicken Quarters, my first real paying job other than baby-sitting.

I tell my friends, when they, of course, ask what my position is, that I am responsible for soliciting business and handing out flyers to passersby while wearing a chicken suit, complete with yellow feathers. Incredulously, they stare at me. When pressed for more details, I decide to spin a yarn, stretching the story to its maximum potential. I continue with incidents that would only happen to someone foolish enough to dress in a hot chicken suit, desperate enough to work the Tuesday night crowd from the racetrack nearby. My friends are enthralled to hear of the particulars of my wild, adventurous job that pays all of two dollars and eighty-five cents an hour. For twenty whole minutes, I keep them engaged with a fabrication that is entertaining even to me. And I know the truth. This is one example of why my friends never quite know if I am being serious or selling an explanation that sounds reasonable, but is hardly fact based. Finally, my interest wanes and I come clean.

"I pack chicken dinners, I make French fries in hot oil, and I greet customers with a warm, approachable smile. Some days I even sell customers things they don't want," I confess to the girls who are agape with interest. Like the time the soda machine went on the fritz because it was running out of carbon to make the soda pop bubbly and we only had access to the root beer button. People rarely order root beer, unless they are under the age of twelve or we are out of Dr. Pepper. But, one afternoon, our toughest customers walked in and it was my turn to work the front register. They are our local police officers. We like to keep them as regulars because our restaurant is right next to the racetrack and around the corner from the city park, where transients go to drink in the dark.

The only thing these officers probably wanted was a beer to chase down their chicken and ribs, but all I had to offer was root beer, so I sold it. "Get your ice-cold root beer, fresh from the fountain, tanks just changed today, and it is oh, so tasty. Can I interest you officers in a trip down memory lane with the finest root beer you've ever tasted? It'll remind you of your childhood on those hot summer afternoons. Have a swig, and if you're not satisfied, the drink's on me."

I was fresh. I was bubbly. And I believed in my product. How could they resist? I am not sure what got in to me. Maybe my dad's salesmanship has rubbed off on me without my knowledge. They looked bemused. I think they bought those two extra large sodas for the sheer pleasure of tantalizing their taste buds with something different for a change. Or maybe they cannot believe that a sixteen-year-old girl is really this enthusiastic about the ice-cold refreshing taste of Mug Root Beer.

"I also avoid cleaning bathrooms, and count back change to customers, badly." I continue listing for my friends the daily grind of my job routine. I get so embarrassed to work the register when there is a rush of people waiting to place their orders. I have patrons who purposely try to confuse me by giving me a five-dollar bill and two cents when clearly their order is only for $4.77. They tell me it is easier this way; they can take a whole quarter back. I am forced to believe them because I can't count backwards in my head. Some days I want to cry.

The last guy who saw the tears beginning to well up in my eyes when I was getting flustered at the mental math he was forcing me to do finally gave up and accepted my three pennies and two dimes as his correct change. I told him to just put the extra two cents he tried to give me back in his pocket. It is just easier for me this way. When my manager saw this exchange, she decided to relieve the pressure of working the front register at night. She put me on day shifts on the weekends, making coleslaw in a garbage barrel with Beula, the old woman who practically lives in the back room. Beula gets paid to keep the secret cole slaw recipe a secret. I don't even get to measure ingredients or know exactly what is in the sauce that makes our 'slaw so sweet. I just have to shred about a hundred heads of cabbage and then dump them into a barrel, where I then mix with my bare hands, up to my elbows, bone chilling mayonnaise and sugar for an hour, until my fingers are blue, or Beula says our 'slaw is done. Very rarely is the 'slaw ever done before my fingers turn blue.

My life as a sixteen-year-old is reserved for social activities that are not usually boasted of in Monday morning Homeroom Advisory. I like to go to the movies with my dad on Friday nights, but my mom gets jealous, so I invite her along, too. This is the only way I can spend more time with my dad, and I figure, in a couple of years, I'll be off to college, so I might as well take advantage of these memory making years now.

When I work a double shift into Saturday night, my friends will sometimes come by and honk the party wagon as they loop through our parking lot. Inevitably, Aileen is driving, because she is the only one of the gang whose parents have a station wagon big enough for cruising with six girls.

While I like my friends a lot, at times they do things that I don't think are very kindhearted. It's not like I really want to say anything to them about their behavior. I just sit by and watch. I guess this makes me just as bad because they think I think they are funny and cool. Mostly, I just think they are a good way to keep my mind off all my problems at home.

No one ever comes to my house. I would be mortified if anyone ever showed up unannounced. I am barely comfortable giving people my phone number because my mother is so unpredictable. I remember a time in seventh grade when I was talking on the phone to Sandy Farnum, a girl I was trying to befriend down the street. We were having a regular girl chat and the usual banter ensued. She told me something far out and my only natural reply was to echo, "Shut Up!" as if to say, "I cannot believe it!"

At the very moment I uttered those two little words, my mother was happening by and smacked me so hard across the face that the receiver reverberated into my ear and cracked along my cheekbone with a thud. We didn't have those modern hand-held phones that were light and portable. Ours was the old-fashioned kind with dead weight in each end of the bulbous mouth and earpiece. The handle was so heavy, the only comfortable way to have a lengthy conversation was to cradle the hook on your neck for support.

In the midst of everything turning upside down in my head, I shakily tried to tell Sandy I had to go for dinner, right away. She asked what was wrong. I told her I just didn't want to keep everyone waiting. I'd call her later, for sure. Before I could run across the room to replace the phone on its cradle, I was letting out a wail and holding my cheek. My face hurt, and my feelings were hurt. I hate being surprised by that backhand.

"Why did you hit me?" I bawled.

"You told me to shut up," she said defiantly.

"I told Sandy to shut up. We were joking around. I didn't even know you were there. I didn't even see you approaching. How could you think I was talking to you? You knew I was on the phone," I tried to rationalize. No amount of logic will work when she gets into one of her states. I just ran to my room and wrote in my journal again how much I want to run away from home. If it weren't for my dad, I'd be gone.

There are times when certain school assignments will come and I can drown myself in them as sort of an escape. Miss Elliott's English class is like this for me on a regular basis. The essay topics she assigns always give me great pause to use my imagination and transport myself to the future: the career I would like to have; what I would do if I found out my best friend was lying to me; or what I would want people to say about me at my funeral. I also love her creative topics that allow me to tell stories with unexpected wry twists, the kind of stories that she would read to the class, and usually they will laugh.

Many days I can find Miss Elliott alone in her room grading papers, and I will stop in to chat for a few minutes. I like her, I really like her. But she is a bit of a strange bird, and most of the girls see her as wacky.

Miss Elliott is very dramatic. She is, in fact, our Drama teacher as well, and her first love is Shakespeare. She has an infatuation with him that practically gets her giddy when she discusses little known facts about his life. She is definitely passionate about his sonnets. Her hair is jet black, and about thirteen shades too dark for her pasty white complexion. She is probably a lot older than she appears. In fact, from a distance at the end of the hall, she looks quite attractive. But the closer you get, the more you find pancake makeup encrusted within the wrinkles that time forgot to erase. Her dramatic black eyeliner, that sweeps outward like Cleopatra's, is a staple. Her mornings begin with ruby red lipstick, but after lunch her classes find crinkly, dry, ruddy lips without a shimmer of Mary Kay color. It really makes a difference. By the end of the day this woman looks haggard. Her jet black hair, that hangs so smoothly in the morning, is all but tattered and recklessly abandoned by the afternoon winds that blow through her convertible on her way to lunch.

I worry about Miss Elliott. I wonder if she has ever married. She strikes me as a person who really only has relationships with cats. Multiple cats. She is quite short, but she loves to wear black go-go boots with everything. They match all of her outfits, because the only colors she will sport are black and white, and of course, the siren red to match the lips. She is very dramatic.

But she is passionate about writing, and her love of English literature is inspiring. She has been kind to me and very generous with the comments she puts on my essays. I am not saying I don't deserve the "As" I get, I just appreciate how much time it must take her to write so many words of praise. Sometimes I get my essays back with a paragraph of notes scrawled in blue felt. I don't see many written remarks on my friends' papers. So I try to be kind to Miss Elliott. But this is hard when everyone considers her to be a bit kooky.

One day, after lunch, she stands in front of class, explaining a new assignment, when she is met with laughter and mockery. The reaction is not one she intends, so she decides, instead, to feel flattered by some seemingly witty remark she must have made. Miss Elliott is explaining the importance of persuasive writing and how mastery of this application will help us when we are writing our college letters for our hopeful acceptance.

Her lecture goes on for some time, but the thing that gets our attention is a fountain pen she is waving in her hand steadily as she emphasizes each point. At one place in her articulation, she motions to her face, to tuck the hair that is sweeping across her lips back to its rightful place behind her ear. She does not realize that her fountain pen has sprung a leak. There is ink all over her index fingers and she has inadvertently smeared cobalt blue across her upper lip, veering slightly right, across her cheek.

The girls behind me notice right away that Miss Elliott has no idea there is ink on her hands. They try to help her along by letting her know that she didn't quite get a morsel of her lunch, which is nestled on the upper corner of her left lip. They speak to her rather hushedly, as if they are doing her a favor by saving her a future embarrassment.

Poor Miss Elliott. She didn't see that one coming. She has now masterfully created the other half of a handlebar mustache with ink she is still oblivious to wearing. The girls are having such a hoot over this that Miss Elliott thinks she is in company with good friends. She continues on with the importance of persuasive writing by giving some examples, while the sniggering cannot manage to stifle itself.

Finally, after ten or fifteen minutes of this bewildering amusement, Miss Elliott retires to her desk with an expression as if to say, "I must be connecting with these girls, after all, I have never seen such gaiety in class." She reminds us that, if we still have questions, to bring our essay idea to her for advice. I have to get to her. I can't stand it any longer. While everyone is settling in and finishing off their parlor joke, I slide through the first two rows to approach Miss Elliott.

In a quiet and very private voice, I tell Miss Elliott, "Your pen has leaked, and it has now accidentally smeared from your fingers to all over your face. I think some of the girls were just not sure how to tell you." I try to be covert. I don't want my friends to know I ratted them out. But I don't want this kind, dingy woman to walk around the rest of the afternoon looking like she made a head dive into a blueberry pie.

"Oh, my goodness gracious." She hurriedly reaches for her pocketbook and slides her hands around until she finds her tiny compact mirror, attached to a silver tube of red lipstick. "I had no idea, girls. This is pretty funny. I didn't know you were trying to trick me into a new makeover. If you don't mind me saying, I know I'm in need of some color, but I think this blue is a little too dark for my skin tone. I was hoping for something in a Tahitian tan." She laughs with them, and every one feels relaxed.

I can't believe it. Miss Elliott isn't mad at all. In fact, she acts as though she is really amused, as if we just played a slumber party trick on her because we like her so much.

I learn today that sometimes when people are trying to make you feel silly, it is important to use a little self-deprecating humor and laugh at yourself. This takes everybody off guard and lowers defenses.

I learn that even the most apparently dingy woman can walk through halls with inner confidence that no one else can detect until you really test her mettle.

I learn that when you let people see the best of you, they really come to like you for who you truly are. If you are comfortable with yourself, it shouldn't matter what other people think of you. Never let others' opinions define you.

Be gracious, be sincere, be unflappable. These qualities will return you safely and happily to your cats, or whatever else might be waiting at home.

Twelfth Grade with Father Downey

Chapter 14

Finally, a senior. This gives us certain rites of passage. The unofficial rule of thumb is that our skirt hems should be hiked one inch for every year. The nuns say it is mandatory that incoming freshman wear their hemlines to their knees, long enough to touch the floor when they are kneeling for mass. By now, senior skirts are short enough to look attractive to all the boys who go by our bus stop after school, screaming obscenities like the common, "Hey, baby, show us some leg." To which we usually wittily respond by pulling down our knee socks. Although the boys find no amusement in this, we can hardly tell because we are laughing with guttural sounds. We are so pleased with our performance. When the boys realize we will not be succumbing to their male wishes, they pass us at the speed of insane teenagers breaking sound barriers in a school zone.

It is a joyous time to be a senior. We even have our own space to hang out downstairs in the basement. All of the lockers and the vending machines are down here, next to the lounge by the pool. Tucked away in the farthest corner of the hall, at the opposite end of the pool, sits the Senior Executive Council room. This is where the Student Body President and all of the other political wannabes convene. It is also where the African-American Student Culture leaders meet. Equally, it serves as headquarters for the Head Cheerleader and her squad, plus the biggest brainiacs and their bookworms.

Each group huddles in this tiny little room, which is really only the size of a large P.E. storage facility for badminton nets and volley-balls. The funny part about being stuffed into this cramped space is that everyone wants to be in here, but nobody really wants to mingle with the other groups. So you will see clusters of girls relegated to their own corners with their in-crowd. No one hardly even advances to any other corner, unless it is, perhaps, to send around a senior vote sheet about some pertinent issue of the week. Should we allow freshmen to go to the dances? Shouldn't seniors be allowed to have an official "cut" day in the spring where we can go have some fun without feeling too guilty about it? Do we think the punishment for the senior prank this year was too harsh?

I don't. Maureen and Aileen, and several of the other girls, decided they were going to sneak into Trinity and go upstairs to the third floor, where the nuns live. They were going to undo the fire hose, and shove it into the nuns' sleeping quarters and turn it on. They thought it would be funny to see a bunch of nuns flying around without their habits. I didn't even get invited to participate because I work at a nice restaurant now on Friday and Saturday nights, so it sort of cuts into a lot of my social life. If I have a special dance I want to go to, I have to give advance notice to get the night off.

But I love my new job as a hostess, and I have finally worked my way up to being Night Hostess for the Upstairs. This is a lot better than being Night Hostess for the Downstairs, because all you get to do is seat people and give them their menus. Upstairs has incredible responsibilities, like answering the phone to take reservations and greeting people as the "ambassador of the restaurant," as my boss puts it. I am the first thing people see when they walk in, and that impression is going to set the whole tone for their evening's experience. We are professional, polished and inviting. I do all of this very well, and I am bubbly, to boot.

So, on this particular prank night, I am working, as usual. The girls figure this will be the case, and decide that the less people who know about the plan, the better. The rumor is that while they were in the middle of unraveling the fire hose, someone accidentally pulled the fire alarm and things got out of hand. The fire hose pressure was so much that the entire upstairs hallway got soaked. The portraits of former graduating classes from the 1930s were not just old, now they were old and mildewed. Some of the teachers' offices were also in harm's way, although there was no real damage done, since most of their work is graded at home.

They never even made it all the way down to the nuns' quarters before the firemen arrived, and Sister Paula came out in her robe. They get in a lot of trouble. But because it is so close to graduation, they don't lose their whole academic achievement. They will still get their diplomas and get to walk across the stage with us. But they also get a hundred hours each of community service, including picking up trash on our West Lawn and gardening the Center Courtyard. While they were embarrassed for about a day, they didn't seem to mind doing any of the penance because I think they thought they were special for having the guts to have gotten into the school after hours and halfway through their plan before getting busted. They figured that they would go down in infamy, and that was good enough for them. I bet anything Maureen's parents were a lot harder on her than any punishment Trinity could have handed out.

Quite frankly, Maureen and I have drifted apart. I have too many issues at home to deal with, and I guess I am just more interested in trying to figure things out by myself. I've pulled away. She knows something isn't right. I can tell. She only asks me everyday, "Why won't you talk to me the way we used to? I'm your best friend. You can tell me anything that's bothering you. Have I done something to bug you?" I just didn't want to get into it. I am different from any other girl in that high school, and I just don't want to lay it all on the table. I've got a weird family. My sister is pregnant, and she is only sixteen. My one brother is smoking pot, and the youngest is in juvenile hall for defacing the American flag by writing "I hate Officer Blum" on it. I don't need all of this spread throughout school.

I really don't know what my future holds. I want to go to college, but my dad says that with the cost of Trinity and braces, all four years, since I wouldn't wear my neck gear to get it over with in eighteen months, that I need to apply to junior college first. Then, if my grades are really outstanding, he will send me to a university for the last two years. My dad retired this year, and I guess that means there isn't as much money coming in as there used to be. I know I should have worn my neck gear, but that is just plain ugly. Fortunately, I look good with braces. They match my dark hair.

My P.M.A. these days isn't very high. My daily objective is to get to school, avoid old friends and finish classes with a level of invisibility that will avoid drawing any unwanted attention my way. I know this is difficult when it is the job of my teachers to get me to participate in class, in life, but I am just trying to handle a lot of things, and I don't want to talk to people.

At least, most people. I reserve a special place in my heart for my first real crush. Oh, he's not one of those teachers with a flare for style, like Mr. Murray, in his cashmere black turtleneck, which offsets his steely good looks. Mr. Murray has the kind of long, wavy brown hair that always appears as if it has been freshly tussled by Ms. Modena's spiky fingernails. He is far too debonair for me. Besides, he and Ms. Modena are the rumored staff couple at the moment. In my opinion, she is a witch whose only talent is being able to roll her Rs in Spanish class.

Mr. Murray is the professor extraordinaire, whose clever comebacks to girls are scrawled across basement lockers to be remembered for the next generation of seniors. The latest is when one girl who was hardly bashful about professing her love to him weekly addressed him as "hon." He could only reply with a deadpanned, "Is that Hun as in Attila, or Hon-ey?" He is a yummy treat. But he is too obvious. I prefer my crushes with a more subtle, less Hollywood quality.

I love Father Downey. Pudgy, smarmy, strict and convertible wheeling Father Downey. He is a literary genius, and I know if I was ever at an adult party with him, we would be off in the corner for hours just talking and laughing. He is the funniest man I have ever known. He, too, has clever quips that become popular statements as girls roam the halls repeating his banter. "Oh, how rude," is this month's catchphrase. It is not just the terminology he uses, it is all in his delivery, as most comedy is. The emphasis is on "rude" and it carries on for longer than its one syllable utterance should require. He is a genius.

I like to participate in his class. But there is a lot that goes unsaid between us, and I wonder if he is thinking the same things. We are currently reading a novel by Charlotte Bronte. I realize that to many she is considered a classic, but she is still not modern enough for me to find the exquisite enjoyment that Father Downey promised. However, we are all immersed in our silent reading and my mind begins to wander. I decide I would rather look at Father Downey than read another word on this page. As I lift my head from my downward glance, I watch him seemingly entranced in his book. The bookmark he uses is a long, rectangular piece of fabric with purple velvet on one side and violet satin on its reverse. A long golden tassel dangling by a braid hangs over the edge of his book while he reads beyond his marker.

I begin to wonder how he has his house decorated. Are there purple pillows thrown everywhere on his couch? Where does he go when he and Mr. Holmes go off campus together, sailing away in his convertible? They always drive with the top down, even on cold days. When they come back, they are in the middle of sharing punch lines and carrying little pink boxes from the bakery tied in string. What did they get that must be so delicious it was good enough to share with the rest of the staff? I want some of that.

In the midst of my wondering, my eyes are met with the most beautiful blue iris' I have seen. Father Downey is gazing at me, as if to hint that I should return to my book. I immediately offer a smile, as if to say, "Yes, I'm reading." I get back to my book until another few minutes go by, and I start to think about Father Downey again. I imagine what it might be like if we could ever date. He'd pick me up in that little Spider convertible, a shade of blue that doesn't do his eyes justice, and we would drive to the ocean.

We would sit on a blanket and eat seafood and listen to the waves crash against the shore. I would tell him why I don't want to talk to any of my friends, and I would tell him about all the problems at my house. I would tell him that I really want to search out my biological roots some day, but I don't want to hurt my dad's feelings. I would admit that I am worried about my future. I don't know what I want to be yet, but I want to make some money so I can move out of my house. I would cry as I begin to tell him that my mother sat on me yesterday. She threw me down on the bed and plopped herself on my stomach, pinning my hands against my sides with her moose thighs.

I don't know what brought this on, but she thought I needed to listen to something she had to say. She weighs two hundred and forty-five pounds. I know this because I looked at her driver's license once to find out what year she was born. She kept on telling my friends that she was a hundred years old, and that got to be embarrassing because some of them believed her. This was when I was in fifth grade. I don't think anyone would believe that now, simply because people don't really live to be that old. I weigh about a hundred and fifteen pounds. She would not get off of me. My brothers were watching and so was my sister. Everyone is afraid of her. I tried to spit in her face to get her to move, but gravity pulled it back like a yo-yo, splattering me beneath my eye. I would tell Father Downey that I need some advice, and maybe he would help.

Father Downey caught me again. This time I was quite sheepish in my gestures and I immediately returned my head to my book. I could feel my face burning and my heart beating faster. He knows I like him. 'What is he doing now?' I wonder. I look again. And Father Downey is waiting with his eyes fixed upon me. We enjoy a mind reading session, until we remember that others in the room might take notice. He puts his spectacles back on, because he always reads with his glasses off. I know this is the signal that class is coming to a close. How is it possible I only read two pages?

My days with Father Downey are numbered. School is winding down, and with only a little over two months to go, my days of harmless flirting are coming to an end. Father Downey is the highlight of my life right now. My other teachers are hard and humorless. The college board is on display in the main entranceway, and all the girls' names who have been accepted to universities around the country are being posted, along with their GPA and the university they will be attending. I know I'm going to junior college, so I don't even apply to my dream schools. I wish I had, just for the fun of it. I wish somebody had told me I could have, even if I didn't plan on attending. Then, at least, I would have letters of acceptance, and a better idea of what my options are.

This depresses me. And what's worse, prom is coming in two

weeks and I don't have a date. My dad has been trying to find out if any of the neighbors have cousins or friends who have sons my age. I am totally mortified when he tells me this, but secretly interested if somebody is going to magically appear as Mr. Tall, Dark and Handsome. It turns out that my buddy Gus, one of the kids I like best out of my parents' circle of friends, will not be gone that week-end with his family, after all. So, problem solved. We'll go together.

When Gus, or Gustav, as my parents like to call him by his given name, arrives, my mother has offered to iron my dress. We bought it at a bridal salon, off the rack, and it is the most beautiful thing I have seen. It has layers of tulle and veil heaped upon a full A-line style skirt. The bodice is fitted with a sprawling tulle ruffle that sweeps diagonally, like a crawling vine, up the single shoulder. This is a dress for a goddess.

It was perfect the way it looked in the store, but my mother believes she can make it look even better. She is a trained seamstress, even though she doesn't sew anymore, and I am happy for her desire to make my prom night special. Gus arrives with a beautiful wrist corsage. He knew to ask me which kind he should get, and I am glad he did, because I could never pin any corsage to the delicate ruffles of tulle on this creation. It would interfere with the ivy-like flow of the pattern. He understood. We hang out for about twenty minutes waiting for my dress to get finished.

"Well, Vandra, you're not going to like what I have to tell you," are the words of doom I hear before I start to feel ill. "Your dress has a hole in it." She is quite succinct.

"It was perfectly fine when we bought it. I'm sure it must be very small. I couldn't see it when I tried it on. It'll be fine." I try to assuage the situation. "Where is the hole?"

"It's in the front. I burned a hole in your dress with the iron. It went right through the top layer of tulle. That iron setting was just too hot." No apologies warranted. It doesn't matter to her that I am crushed and my dream dress is ruined. I look at Gus and the tears start to well in my eyes. I run into my room, intending to flop down on my bed and suffocate myself in my imitation goose down pillow. Before I can slam the door behind me, I slug out the words, "We're not going to the prom! Everything's ruined!"

Gus is a good one. My father always says he has integrity. I was not sure what the word meant at first until it was explained that Gustav is someone my dad trusts with me. Whenever we go out, my dad knows I will be safe. Gus always makes it a point to get me home before my curfew and usually comes in to watch a little TV or make popcorn. There are plenty of times when he has slept over at our house because he lives sort of far away, and then he will go to church with us the next day.

Gus knows our family pretty well. He is the only person I have ever invited into my house during all of high school. I remember one time he and I were sitting on the couch in the family room watching a little TV after dinner. The kitchen and the family room are all mingled together, no walls. The television sits on top of the counter, so we can experience the joy of family. My mom went into one of her tirades, which she likes to do whenever there is company over. I may have learned my lesson a long time ago about inviting guests to the house, but my siblings were always having people in, so there were many occasions for her to put on a little show.

This one particular scene started like all the other great opening acts, with a pot and pan dance. The kitchen was her main stage because she could do so much damage and make so much noise that she knew she could not be ignored. There Gus and I sat quietly, immovably frozen, eyes glued to the television, when the real drama was unfolding in the open theater just behind the TV. She started screaming about something crazy, and lids were getting clanged and pans were being thrown and the chrome sink was taking its beating. Gus maintained his eyes on forward lock on the TV and only moved his lips slightly when he mumbled, "This is not my family. These are not my problems."

This would have been humiliating if I heard these words coming from any other person, but from Gus-Gus, it was hilarious. His straight-faced delivery and lack of reaction to the hysteria that was my regular after-dinner treat made me feel like I could laugh, rather than cry. So, Gus is no stranger to the madness that lives inside my house.

He finally knocks on my bedroom door. My dad said it was okay for him to come talk to me, making an exception to the strict "no boys in the back of the house" rule. I let him in.

"She did it on purpose, you know. She never wants me to be happy. I don't want to go to the prom. Everyone will laugh at me." I begin to cry some more.

"It's okay, Vanny. We don't have to go. We can go to the movies instead, or I can drive us to dinner, and then we can just come home. It's whatever you want to do. Tonight is your night." He is always so reassuring.

"But you're in a tux and you spent all this money. I feel bad that you have to come over here when she is always being weird."

"It doesn't bother me. You're not weird. You're great. I like spending time with you. If this is the only way I can do that, then it's okay with me. Believe me, my family has its problems too. Not like this," he says with that Cheshire cat grin that only makes me smile back, "but every family has their issues. Don't let it get you down."

I begin to feel a little better. At least I'm feeling like I want to take another good long look at that dress. It sounded pretty bad, but can it be fixed, is what I am wondering now. "Will you go get that dress and bring it here? I want to see how bad it is."

"I'll go, but Vanny, it's not looking too good. There is a hole through the first two layers, and the fabric has melted. There are pieces sticking straight up that might cut you if you touch it. It looks like she steamed that thing with a bucket of acid." He was trying to make me laugh, but I had an idea that might work.

It was a quick flash of a moment for him to dash down the hall to get the dress from the sewing room, which is what we now call the former bedroom that my sister used to sleep in before she went off to Reno to get married to that stupid boy. Just as I thought, the dress looks the same from the front or the back. Who will ever really know just how bad the dress looks in pictures if I turn it around and put the off shoulder single tulle ivy drape on my right shoulder instead of on my left? So this is what I decide to do. Without another minute to waste, I make a beeline to the bathroom to redo my makeup and fix the hair that has been buried in my pillow for the past fifteen minutes.

Gus tells me later that he is proud of me for thinking of such a clever way to turn things around, because he really is looking forward to going to prom with me. He tells me again that everything will turn out all right and not to worry. My dad is right; Gus-Gus is a good one.

Several weeks later, school is coming to a close and girls are crying in the halls because they won't see each other ever again. Of course, they'll see one another every day for the next three weeks, when, after that, it'll be on to summer, where they'll probably spend every night together as they count down the time they have left until they depart for college. But right now, everybody's crying. Ugh!

I am feeling equally out of sorts because I started off high school with my best friend Maureen, and now I have botched things so badly with her that we don't even talk. The girls I introduced her to are now more her friends than mine, and I hang out with a girl named Trish, who has been scorned from the Executive Council Room merely because she doesn't fit into any of the groups, and could care less about it. I'd like to be more like Trish, confident on the inside, strong in my opinions, and able to look somebody in the face who is talking about me behind my back and tell them exactly what I think of them.

Father Downey is Assistant Principal for the week because Mrs. Vender's mother died and she had to go back to Massachusetts for the funeral and to take care of some family business. I am scurrying up the basement staircase to get to the second floor library so I can finish studying for my test in two hours when I pass Father Downey heading in the opposite direction toward Mrs. Vender's office, where he's been making himself comfortable.

"Hey, Vandra, where are you going right now?" he asks with the same sort of inquisitiveness that my friends do when they are trying to find out what I'm doing Friday night. Regardless of what I say, it won't really matter because the point is they have something better in mind for me. So I take the bait.

"Well, I'm supposed to be studying for a test in Spanish, but I pretty much know the words. I just wanted to review. But I have a lot of time this study hall, so I'm pretty flexible right now." I hoped that sounded like I was interested if, indeed, he did have something better in mind, other than casual hall conversation.

"Do you want to see the prom pictures? They just came in and no one knows they're here yet. Come on. We can go make fun of all the ugly dresses and the bad-looking prom dates." This was more fun than sitting around drawing stretch marks and mustaches on super models in my teen magazines.

"Oh, yes. Let's go!" The "s" in my "yes" just hisses with glee and delight. We amble down that hallway faster than two people racing to get the last cookie off the snack cart in the cafeteria. We don't even sit in chairs. Father Downey sits on the platform step that creates a sort of high-rise for Mrs. Vender's desk area and guest chairs. When you are in serious trouble, you land up there. When she is hosting parents and having meetings, you are in the sunken parlor of her office, where there are two couches and tree plants beside each coffee table.

We sit upon the glossy hardwood floor and pull over the big box from the photographers Milton and Housen. They get all our school business. They even did my senior portraits. "Look at this. It's Julie Farrantino. Well, isn't she just the belle of the ball in her southern dress. She looks like Scarlett O'Hara. Why didn't she just take down the curtain rods while she was at it and make shoulder pads?"

I can't believe it. Father Downey is getting campy about our head cheerleader. I knew he was funny in class, but I didn't know he was this funny outside of class. He thinks the same things we all think about the cheerleaders. Who has cheerleaders at an all-girls school anyway?

Father Downey starts pulling out the best "bad photos" and letting the comments rip. He is fast on his feet, and he makes fun of boys in their burgundy tuxes with pink ruffled shirts and pink carnations. "Who buys pink carnations for boutonnieres? He probably isn't going out with her ever again." He called that one right. The guy was a jerk, anyway, but Annie Poulter was a bigger jerk. He even left her at the prom to go home with Aileen. I had to share this with Father Downey because he seems to be totally into this kind of gossip.

We sit here for ninety minutes of my study hall, just laughing and poking fun at some of the meanest girls in high school. When he sees Maureen's picture he notices that she got her hair permed in time for the big formal. "Going with the fresh poodle look, are we?" I feel relaxed and better than I have in months. I finally get some time alone with my favorite teacher and we get to make fun of some of the people who don't talk to me anymore.

I don't know how much he notices about my social life, but when he gets to my picture with Gus, all he offers me is a sincere, "Your dress looks beautiful, Vandra. And ever since you got your braces off, your smile has never been more radiant. You have a bright future ahead of you, and I just know good things will happen for you. Just keep a little faith that you are doing what is right, and it will all work out. People look to you as an example, even though you might not think so. And your teachers genuinely like you. You will always be one of my favorite students." He gives me a little wink and closes up the box. "Promise, you won't tell anyone we were in here making fun of people's pictures." He says it with a boyish grin. He knows he can trust me, but I promise anyway, and I mean it. No one will ever hear it from me.

With that, it is over. I have to go to my next class, and Father Downey has done his good work for the day. I walk out of there feeling like I can touch the sun.

I learn today that Father Downey has a way of making people feel special. He is in tune with me when I am at my lowest. I learn that a friendly smile from across a room full of silent readers can get me to take my mind off my troubles. A wink from him and a secret pact make me feel like we have a special alliance. All of a sudden it is more important to just be with someone who likes my company than it is for me to unload all my baggage and then have him know how weird my life really is. I learn that the simple pleasure of sitting with someone I can trust, who trusts me, to make fun of some people I do not trust anymore is a very soothing exchange.

I learn from Father Downey that there are crushes in life. Sometimes we can't do anything about them but just enjoy them from afar. Sometimes just knowing the other person feels the same way is enough comfort to get you to the next day. Father Downey is my something to look forward to on most days in my senior year. I learn from him what it means to notice people who might not want to be noticed. And finding a way to make those people feel like they matter is a special quality to have and a special gift to receive. Father Downey is a generous spirit. I hope I remember to pass his lessons along when I encounter others.

Check "Yes" or "No"

Chapter 15

There is a penetrating silence in the room that I have only heard once before. It was at a wedding, when the ice sculpture that beautifully captured the bride and groom melted all over the dance floor because it was too close to the "charming" fireplace the bride insisted on having for her winter wonderland theme. I have only associated this kind of silence with the doom and despair that seem to follow next.

Have I said too much? Mrs. Sanders is staring at me with a look I cannot read. Her pen has not moved since we began this interview. It remains poised in her delicate hand. Her legs have not uncrossed once in the time it has taken me to recount my lessons learned. Even her linen suit, with all its starch, has held up nicely through our session. Have I touched her? Is she moved? Does she now believe that I am suitable to raise a child? How many tests do other parents have to pass in order to get that certificate saying they are now ready to be outstanding parents and raise outstanding children?

My friends all figured it out the hard way. And they have children who laugh and giggle and fall asleep during bedtime stories every night. Even the times when their children cry because they have fallen down the steps or burned themselves on the hot stove for the first time or climbed up on a counter they couldn't get down from without landing on their head, my friends soon realized this is how you learn to parent. It is in the action of doing, not in the passive reading.

"Mrs. Sanders, I feel like I have been talking for an awfully long time. Did I answer your question? Do you have a better sense of the kind of person I am by the experiences I have gained from my own childhood?" With every question I am tentative, hoping that she will soon respond. I pause before I ask another. "I hope that you and the agency will find that I am, indeed, ready to take on this awesome responsibility of raising a child. I am anxious for your feedback."

"Ms. Zandinski, Vandra, if I may, I hardly know what to say. You have shared with me some very important lessons that some adults do not even come to understand in their wiser years. At one point, I wondered if the scars from the experiences with your difficult mother would somehow be manifested in raising your own daughter."

Oh, no. My heart begins to sink. Trying to anticipate her final decision, my head starts to spin with thoughts. Please don't think that I am scarred by my childhood. I tell you this story so you will take away all the positives I gained from having to experience difficult trials. I know my mother was limited in her ability to mother. I don't bear any malice toward her for her shortcomings. I feel lucky that I had a dad who more than made up for her lack of maternal instincts. Please don't hold this against me.

She continues. "But the more I listened to all the really strong people you had in your life to help guide you and bring you confidence, the more I realized that your experience is very synonymous with what we try to achieve through adoption. Our belief is that sometimes a family is found in the people who buoy you and stick by you and love you through life-changing events. Family is where you find it, and that is not always in the genes."

I am beginning to like the sound of this. "Yes, I agree. I have always said that just because you are raised with different people under the same roof, it does not necessarily make you a family. Sometimes that collection of individuals never really forges a bond."

"Vandra, I would like to say that I think you will make a terrific parent one day. Any child would be lucky to have you as their Mommy. Of course, we still have two more interviews that will need to be passed before I can send my recommendation to the board. I will need to interview your husband to find out what he will contribute as a father, and then I'll invite you back together so we can see how you interact with one another. The one thing I will be curious to know in your couple interview is a little bit of your history together. How did you and your husband meet? Tell me about your relationship and why you will make a good home for one of our children?"

And now it's over. The calendar is perused, the appointment is set. In one month I will have to explain why I chose to marry this man and why, together, we will be outstanding parents.

How will I ever put into words to a complete stranger the reasons I actually decided to exchange vows with Grant Santistevan and have it come out making sense, when it doesn't even make sense to me now. I have one month to think this through. I need to take a nap. Then I'll be able to figure out what I need to say. This is agony.

Questions for Discussion

1) A "life lesson" is a pivotal teaching moment where one of the secrets to getting through life's obstacles is revealed. Every single person learns these lessons, but not at the same stage in their lives. In your opinion, what is the most significant lesson Vandra has learned that will best prepare her for adulthood?

2) Think of some people you know who always seem to be getting commendations and special recognition. What traits do these people have in common? Is Vandra an "underdog" or a "winner"? Justify your interpretation by first defining each term in your own words and then identifying the qualities she possesses to support your answer.

3) In Vandra's earliest education at Montessori, she learns that there are different categories of "independent thinkers". Among our role models made famous through history or pop culture, who would you assign into each of the three categories of independent thinkers Vandra delineates and describes?

4) What is your earliest memory of school? What was the first experience to shape your "joy of learning?" When was the first moment you decided you either had a love for reading or a dislike of it?

5) Was Vandra's mother right or wrong for writing her daughter's state report in Miss Ryan's fifth grade class? From Vandra's mother's point of view, why do you think she believes she is helping

her daughter? Vandra learns "the experience of our plight is lesson enough." What does this phrase mean to you?

6) Loyalty and friendship is a recurring theme throughout this story. The connection between Vandra and Kirsten illustrates that good friends are priceless. What drew them together? Describe the time when you knew a friend would do anything for you.

7) The lesson "Escape routes and backup plans are necessary to avoid evil trappings" can be useful in many situations besides running from bullies. Identify at least <u>three</u> other scenarios where this rule can apply. How can students work together to effectively prevent harassment?

8) Role-play. If you were Mr. Koker, the seventh grade Science teacher, how would you handle Vandra's new attitude? Rewrite his monologue and deliver it orally, animatedly reenacting his wrath.

9) What do you think Mrs. Schreiber is really trying to teach Vandra by not accepting her late paper and posting her note on the wall for all to read?

10) Strict high school teacher Mr. Harris is a pivotal character who epitomizes for Vandra the idea that life is precious and to treat people as if there's no tomorrow. Do you view him as a protagonist or antagonist? Relate the qualities that make him both and then make a case for your final argument in favor of one. Is he truly the antagonist, or merely an excellent teacher who holds students highly accountable for learning?

11) Of all the teachers illustrated in each chapter, which type(s) have you experienced in your own education? What are the life lessons you learned from them?

12) What do you think is the single most difficult trial Vandra faces in this book? When do you think she is rewarded for her efforts?

13) Understanding another person's point of view prevents conflicts. Write a back story for the character of Vandra's mother. Evaluate two scenarios when Vandra is let down by something her mother says and make Vandra's mother a sympathetic character. Provide detailed insight as to what hardships in her own childhood may have taken place to shape the adult she has become.

14) The secondary story line of Vandra as an adult trying to adopt fleshes out the theme that "family is where you find it." Is this true? Can you create deeper bonds with people who are not blood relatives? Also, can it be possible that people living under the same roof really never connect? Have you ever had a mother figure in your life who wasn't your mother? What is your definition of "family?"

15) Project into the future. How does Vandra's relationship with her mother evolve? Does she ever forge a bond with her and, if so, what events help propel this? How does Vandra's life move on beyond high school? At the reunion in ten years, what happens when Vandra meets all of her teachers again? Who does she maintain as friends for life?